Praise for *Mercy: The Last New England Vampire*

"A beautifully told tale of supernatural folklore and ancestry that ends in a terrifying thrill ride readers can sink their teeth into."

—Amanda Marrone, bestselling author of *Devoured*

In her novel, Mercy: The Last New England Vampire, *Sarah Thomson got it right. Unlike so many other young adult vampire novels that cannot escape the fanged shadow of the fictional Dracula, Mercy is firmly grounded in the historical reality of vampires. It is clear that the novel's main character, Haley, understands that Mercy was a scapegoat and that it was fear of a mystifying illness that drove Mercy's family to perform a horrific ritual. As Haley so poignantly says of Mercy, "this wasn't a horror movie ... It was her life."*

—Michael Bell, author of *Food for the Dead*

"Sarah Thomson's *Mercy weaves the dark threads of an old New England legend into a contemporary tale of ghostly mystery that is both compelling and genuinely chilling. In a literary genre overrun with sparkling vampires and romance-novel angst, Thomson has crafted a welcome return to the shadowy terrors of graves and ghouls. I found myself unable to put the book down. A deliciously eerie way to pass a stormy night!"*

—Christopher Rondina, author of *Vampires of New England*

MERCY

THE LAST
NEW ENGLAND
VAMPIRE

SARAH L. THOMSON

Other fiction titles from Islandport Press

Billy Boy
by Jean Flahive

Contentment Cove and *Young*
by Miriam Colwell

Windswept, Mary Peters, and *Silas Crockett*
by Mary Ellen Chase

Available from
www.islandportpress.com

MERCY

THE LAST NEW ENGLAND VAMPIRE

SARAH L. THOMSON

ISLANDPORT PRESS • YARMOUTH

ISLANDPORT PRESS
P.O. Box 10
Yarmouth, Maine 04096
www.islandportpress.com
books@islandportpress.com

ISBN: 978-1-934031-36-0
Library of Congress Card Number: 2011925633

Front and back cover photos: Sarah L. Thomson
Author photo: Mark Mattos
Book jacket design: Karen Hoots / Hoots Design
Book design: Michelle Lunt / Islandport Press
Publisher: Dean Lunt

To Ann, Melissa, and Kirsten—Mercy's first fans
—S.L.T.

CHAPTER ONE:
MERCY

I woke that morning with blood on my pillow. Red blossoms on white linen, like roses in snow.

It was starting for me. Just as it had started for my mother and my sister.

Downstairs, I could hear Edwin coming in from the barn, carrying a bucket of fresh warm milk to the kitchen. Like any eight-year-old boy, he banged the door behind him. The sound of his voice filled the house to bursting. His spirits were exhausting. They sapped the heat from my veins.

But I was glad to hear him, all the same. When it was over for me, my father would still have his son to love.

The thought of my father made me rise from my bed, determined to wash the pillowcase before he could see. But I was suddenly dizzy from the effort of standing upright. And I caught sight of myself in the looking glass. My pale face drifted in the depths of the mirror like a drowned woman floating through fathoms of black, cold water.

I could tell. It wouldn't be long now.

CHAPTER TWO:
HALEY

"That's where they burned her heart." Haley pointed toward a low stone wall that ran along the edge of the Chestnut Hill Cemetery. "Right there."

Melanie twisted her mouth and made a noise that sounded like *yurghch*. "Burned her heart? Why?"

"Because that's what you do with vampires."

"I thought you drove a stake though their hearts," Mel objected. "That's what they always do on *Buffy*."

Haley shrugged, getting out her camera. "Maybe vampires in Rhode Island are different. Anyway, that's what they did." She crouched down, holding the digital camera out, tilting it to try different angles. The pale slab of marble, leaning a little, centered itself in the screen and she took the photo—dirty white stone, faded grass shaggy at its feet, the late autumn sky, a chilly blue, distant behind it. The simple letters on the stone were sharp, in crisp focus. MERCY L. BROWN. DAUGHTER OF GEORGE T. & MARY E. BROWN. DIED JAN. 18, 1892. AGED 19 YEARS.

Haley switched the camera over to black-and-white. Now the image in the viewscreen looked eerie. She stopped the

3

exposure down to darken it a little. A scene from an old horror movie. All it needed was a werewolf to come around the corner.

"So why did they think she was a vampire? And dig her up and everything?" Mel had perched on another headstone to wait.

Haley took the second photo and then backed up to get a wider shot, including the stone wall, the old graves surrounding Mercy's, a willow, bare of leaves, leaning as if it were cold, turning away from the wind.

"They didn't dig her up. She wasn't buried yet. She was in that crypt over there." The crypt was against the far wall of the cemetery, a low stone building with brush hanging over the sloping roof. It looked as if it had been dug into a hill rather than built up from the ground. "And they did it because people were dying." Haley clicked the shutter, took a step, clicked again. "Tuberculosis. Consumption, that's what they called it."

"Consumption. That sounds so romantic." Mel laid the back of her hand across her forehead and sighed. "Beautiful ladies, wasting away, leaving their heartbroken lovers behind . . . "

"Coughing up little bits of their lungs," Haley said without looking up from the camera. She switched it back to color. She wanted a wide-angle shot. All those gravestones.

She heard the toughness in her own voice as she answered Mel. Like it didn't bother her at all, the thought of somebody dying like that.

Nineteen. Mercy had only been five years older than Haley. Four years younger than . . .

All those gravestones. The picture in her viewscreen wobbled a little.

"It's not romantic," she said sharply, lowering the camera without taking the shot. "Mercy's mom and her older sister died of it before she did."

The graves of Mercy's mother, Mary, and Mary's oldest daughter, Grace, were close by. This spot in the cemetery was full of Browns. The headstones went back more than a century. None of them were big and elaborate. Elsewhere in the cemetery there were crypts, carved tombs, statues of angels, cherubs. But the Browns just had names and dates. The most you could say for Haley's ancestors was that there were a lot of them. And that they stayed put. There had been Browns in Rhode Island for hundreds of years.

"Yeah, I know." Mel gave Haley an apologetic look. "I just—"

"And then her little brother got sick too." Haley knew she shouldn't snap at Mel. She tried to get some lightness back in her voice. "Of course, that was the problem."

"What was?"

"That her brother got sick. Right after she died." Haley turned off the camera and stuffed it back in the pocket of her red fleece jacket. "That's why they took her out of the crypt. And cut her open."

Tough, Haley told herself. *Like it doesn't matter. Like you don't care.* Anything to make Mel stop with that look. That "I'm sorry," look. That "I understand, you're dealing with so much," look.

This time Mel made a sound like *erck*.

"And when they found fresh blood in her heart, that was it. They decided she was a vampire."

"That's really disgusting."

"Not as disgusting as what they did with the ashes of her heart."

"What?"

"You don't want to know. It's too disgusting."

"Ha-ley!"

"Okay, okay." *A joke. It's all a joke.* "They mixed the ashes with water or something and gave it to her little brother to drink."

"That is so *disgusting!*"

"I told you."

With the camera back in her pocket, Haley began to feel nervousness creep over her. It started in her feet. Restless, they wanted to move. Then it began to sneak up her spine. Without the distraction of a picture to arrange—light and shadow, shape and angle, color and pattern aligning themselves in the viewscreen—the quiet of the cemetery began to press in on her. With all those trees and bushes and clumps of straggly grass, you'd think there would be crows cawing, squirrels chattering, little things rustling in the dry dead leaves. But there was nothing, not even traffic on the road that ran by the gate.

"So did it work?"

"Work?"

Mel rolled her eyes. "The *ashes*. Did it work? Did her brother get better?"

"Of course he didn't." Now the restlessness had moved to Haley's hands. She rubbed at her short red hair, scratched the back of her neck. Then she shoved her hands into her pockets. Her fingers curled around the little metal box of her camera, cool and solid. It felt good to have something to hold. "He had tuberculosis. He needed antibiotics, not the ashes of his sister's heart. His grave's right over there."

Mel hopped up and went over to look at the small headstone. Strands of her dark brown hair slipped loose from her braid to fall around her thoughtful face. "Edwin Brown. Haley, look. He was just a kid."

"I know. He was eight. Come on, Mel, let's go. I've got everything I need."

But Mel, crouched on her heels before the grave, didn't get up. She reached out a hand to lightly touch the shallow letters of Edwin's name, blurred by time. "That's so sad."

"Mel, come *on*."

"What's with you?"

6

"Nothing. I'm fine." She was fine. Except the sun was dipping down toward the tops of the trees. The late afternoon light was the best for photography; that was why the two of them were here now. But it meant that sunset was closer than Haley felt comfortable with when she was surrounded by graves. And *that* was why she'd asked Mel to come with her.

Like a little kid, Haley told herself scornfully. *Scared to go to a cemetery alone. Scared of the dark.*

She was relieved when Mel got up. But when her friend started walking, it was in the wrong direction. Away from the gate.

Haley bit back a groan and followed her.

A few minutes later, Mel had found what she was looking for. She stood over a grave, much more recent than Mercy's, and pulled something out of her pocket: a little plastic package of soup crackers. She opened it, crumbled the crackers in her hand, and let the crumbs drift down over the grass.

Haley stared at her.

"Gran loved birds," Mel said, crunching up her second handful of crackers. "I always bring something for the birds when I come to visit her."

"Oh. Okay." Haley hadn't known that. She hadn't known that Mel liked to visit her grandmother's grave at all.

How long had it been? Three years ago? Haley had come to the funeral. She remembered Mel's white, pinched face, and the way Mel's mother had looked as if she were sleepwalking. As if grief had made her too tired to stand.

"She could even tell the different kinds of sparrows apart. Not many people can do that."

"Uh-huh." Haley watched the bits of cracker falling, like snow, from Mel's hand. You couldn't exactly say, "Hurry up, could you?" to a friend at her grandmother's graveside, but still. Still. The sunlight was starting to fade.

7

Even though Haley was very carefully and very patiently not saying anything at all, Mel looked over at her quizzically.

"I'm fine," Haley said quickly. "I just—this place creeps me out. A little."

"Really?" Mel brushed crumbs off her hands. Then, to Haley's relief, she started walking at last. "It doesn't bother me," she went on. "I mean, it's sad, kind of, but it's—ow!"

Mel's foot had caught on a thin, orange nylon rope, snaking through the grass. It had been pegged down at four corners to make a neat rectangle at the end of a row of graves.

Haley looked down on it. A new one. Someone was going to come here and dig a new grave.

"Peaceful," Mel finished, shaking her foot loose. "You know? Like everybody's sleeping."

A new one. A fresh grave. One more to add to the hundreds and hundreds already here.

"Let's just go, okay?" Haley's voice was brittle as thin ice.

Mel's face said *Sure, whatever.*

Peaceful, Haley thought angrily. Walking as quickly as she could without looking like she was trying to walk quickly, she made her way between rows of graves back toward the gate. That was the kind of stupid word people used about cemeteries. People who didn't want to admit what a place like this actually was.

Even Mel didn't understand. She could look at all those graves, at her own *grandmother's* grave, and think *peaceful.* As if she didn't know that every stone stood for a death.

Stood for somebody gone. A life taken away. And now there would be a new grave, and somebody else would be lowered into it, covered with dirt, weighed down, trapped. Forever.

"It's funny, though," Mel said, breaking into Haley's thoughts.

8

"Hysterical," Haley agreed. The gate was right over there. "I'll have Samuelson rolling in the aisles."

"Don't be stupid. I mean, fresh blood in her heart?" For a minute, Mel looked as spooked as she had in the days when she'd slept over at Haley's and Haley would insist on reading ghost stories out loud once the house was dark and quiet. After a while her mom had confiscated all her spooky books. "I mean, how could that happen? She'd been dead for, like, months? Right?"

"Well, it didn't happen because she was coming back from the dead to suck the life out of her little brother!" Haley snapped.

"I *know*. It's just creepy, don't you think?"

"I really don't." Ten more feet. Five. Haley let out a silent breath of relief as they stepped under the wrought-iron gateway.

"You're so going to get an A on this project. It's not fair." Mel bent over to fiddle with the lock on her bike. "Samuelson should think before he gives these assignments out. I mean, not everybody has an interesting ancestor."

"You've got a Civil War veteran," Haley pointed out.

But it was true. *Samuelson better be impressed with this project,* she thought to herself. After all, how many kids in his American history class could claim a real, live—maybe she should say real, dead—vampire in their family trees?

And Haley needed a good grade. If she brought home a D or an F for the semester, even her dad and Elaine would probably notice. This "Research an Ancestor" project could save her GPA. She had to show Samuelson she was trying.

He'd talked to her after that last test. Was she having trouble studying? Could he help with any of the material? Did she want to see the counselor?

He'd been concerned. Nice. Everybody was nice lately. It was starting to drive Haley crazy. She would rather Samuelson had yelled. If he'd been mean, she could have gotten angry, and anger helped these days. Nice just brought her perilously close to tears.

"Let's go into town," Mel proposed, pulling on her bright orange gloves. "We can get a hot chocolate or something."

"Can't."

"Oh, come on, Haley. You couldn't do anything last weekend and now—"

Haley shook her head. "Can't. I have to go see Jake."

CHAPTER THREE:

HALEY

When Haley opened the door to Jake's apartment, a whirlwind of golden fur nearly knocked her down. Jake's golden retriever whined and barked, leaped up to put her two front paws on Haley's chest, then flung herself away to dash around the room, bouncing from wall to wall in a frenzy of pleasure.

"Well, we know who the popular one around here is." Jake's friend Liam looked up from his handful of cards. "Hey, Haley." He waved a hand at her and the cigarette tucked between his fingers trailed a thin line of smoke through the air.

"Take her out, take her out." Jake was sprawled in the big armchair by the window, feet propped up on a footstool. "Or she might go right through a wall."

Haley carefully avoided looking at Liam as she mumbled hello and grabbed Sunny's leash from the hook by the door. He was too good-looking, blond and tall with his soul patch and his dark-rimmed glasses and his air of disdainful amusement, as if the world were a mildly entertaining joke. Mel got giggly around him, but Haley tried to avoid talking to him directly. He made her feel shy and stupid and extremely young.

"See you and call," Liam said as Haley made Sunny stand still long enough to clip the leash onto her collar. "You're bluffing. You don't have a thing."

"How can you doubt a man in my condition?" Jake asked reproachfully. Plastic poker chips clattered softly on the table beside his armchair.

Liam snorted. "Wouldn't surprise me if you make the whole thing up just to get more money out of my pocket. Or to get girls, probably. The sympathy card. God knows they wouldn't look at you any other way. Look how you got your poor little cousin there walking your dog for you."

When Sunny heard the metal clasp of her leash snick closed, she dashed out the door, dragging Haley behind her down the long hallway.

"Run a marathon with her, why don't you?" Jake's voice drifted out after her. "It might calm her down."

Sunny sniffed her way down the street, sticking her nose into every bush and investigating every street sign and fire hydrant. Haley had to zip up her jacket, pulling the sleeves down over her hands as the dark started to gather, tangling like smoke in the branches of the bare trees. Not even five o'clock and the day was already over. November had to be the worst month of the year. All the brilliance of fall was fading away and there was nothing but months of cold stretching out ahead, blank and white and bare. Even the promise of Christmas was not enough to make up for it. And as for Thanksgiving . . .

At last Sunny's nervous energy was worked off and the dog stopped pulling at the leash, settling into an easy pace by Haley's side. They walked till they reached East Park, a triangular scrap of worn-out grass with a few swings and a battered slide. A couple of little kids were still playing. Haley watched as one pumped her swing up high and then leaped off, flinging herself forward. She landed hard and fell to her hands and knees, but she was laughing, triumphant.

Haley remembered doing that. She and Mel, back in second grade, every recess, racing across the playground to get the swings first. There was that moment when you let go of the chains, just at the peak of your swing, and you could soar. It was amazing.

She couldn't do it now. Haley had tried, once or twice, but she'd grown too much. Too heavy. She could swing, but she couldn't fly.

She turned the dog back toward Jake's. Sunny trotted quietly now, glancing up at Haley every now and then with a mixture of affection and anxiety. *You're still there, right?* Haley imagined the dog thinking, *Oh, good. You're still there, right?*

"Not going anywhere," she whispered, and reached down to stroke Sunny's head gently.

When they got back, Liam was shrugging into his jacket. Jake hadn't moved. The cards were scattered up on the table by his chair, poker chips lying around them. Sunny waited, quivering impatiently, for Haley to take off the leash, then dashed over to bury her head in Jake's lap. He pulled her ears, smiling down at her, and she made a happy mooing sound. It was her way of greeting him. Sunny knew better than to jump on Jake.

Haley slipped her camera out of her pocket. Quickly, before either of them could move, she snapped the picture—Sunny's smooth golden head, her dark eyes lifted up to stare at Jake, the affection in Jake's fingers as he ruffled her fur.

"That's six hundred and seventy-three dollars you owe me, you deadbeat," Liam announced. "Haley, you're a witness."

"I'll leave it to you in my will. Anyway, I should deduct something for all of my beer you drink."

Liam was tall enough that he would have towered over Jake, if Jake had stood up. He lifted weights, or ran triathlons, or something, Haley couldn't remember, when he wasn't directing plays. His voice was deep and loud, an actor's voice, trained to project to the back row of seats. Next to him Jake seemed even more frail than usual.

Liam pulled his keys from a pocket and fiddled with them. "The play's opening next Friday," he said after a moment, and Haley thought it was the first time she'd ever seen him look awkward. "If you—I mean, the set looks great. If you think you can make it . . . "

Jake smiled with one corner of his mouth.

"Probably not. But thanks."

"Well. Call. If you change your mind."

Jake nodded and Liam left quickly, looking (Haley thought) relieved. He aimed to ruffle her hair on the way out, but she ducked. Her lips pinched in disapproval as she saw the two green bottles he'd left on the floor. She picked them up and set them near the door so she could take them to the recycling bin on the way out. Didn't he know better than to leave a thing like that for Jake to finish?

And didn't he know better than to ask Jake to do something he couldn't? As if Jake was remotely well enough to go out to a play, even to see the last set he'd designed. Before he got sick. Again.

"It stinks in here," she muttered as she began to stack the poker chips in their box.

"He only smoked one, Haley." Jake sounded a little amused. "His weekly cigarette. He always saves it for the game. Leave that stuff, I'll do it later. You're not the maid."

"How do you play poker anyway?" Haley asked, to distract him, as she continued to sort the little red and white and blue discs. They fell neatly into their places with a satisfying plastic clicking sound. Next to the chips and the cards on the table was an ashtray where Jake often dumped pencils and pens. Right now it held smudges of dark gray ash and the butt from Liam's cigarette.

Jake looked horrified. "You don't know?" Haley shook her head. "Your education has been sadly lacking. Seriously, I never taught you this? Sit down."

Haley hesitated, looking sharply at Jake's face, trying to gauge the pallor of his skin. Were the circles under his eyes darker than usual? He'd already had one visitor today. "I don't know. I should go. You're—"

"I can rest in the grave, so they tell me." Haley winced, but Jake had already picked up the cards and was starting to shuffle them. "Sit. Get me a piece of paper. Here are the hands. One pair's the lowest, you never bet much on one pair. Then two . . ."

Haley sat. The lamp, shining over Jake's shoulder, cast a warm yellow circle of light on the table where he was slapping down the cards. The rest of the room was in dimness, including the hospital bed against the far wall, the dresser with comb and hairbrush and the clusters of small brown plastic bottles.

Jake handed out chips—the whites were one, the reds were five, the blues ten—and showed Haley how to ante, tossing two white chips onto the table. Then he dealt.

"Five-card draw," Jake said, a little breathless from so much talking. "Pick up your hand, look at it, see if you have any of those things I wrote down for you."

"A pair of sevens."

Jake groaned. "Don't tell me, stupid. Never mind. I didn't hear that. Now we bet. Then you tell me how many new cards you want and we bet again."

After Haley had lost several hands dismally, she began to catch on. "Heard from your mom?" Jake asked as he shuffled and dealt once more.

"Yeah. Thanksgiving in Manhattan."

"That'll be good, right?"

Haley raised her eyes to Jake's face in disbelief. "Remember last year? She ordered in Thai food."

Jake grinned. "Aunt Kay was never a traditionalist. I'll bet five. But why not? Pad thai is something to be thankful for."

"This year she wants to try *Ethiopian*. See you. Is that right?"

"That's right. Well, what's wrong with Ethiopian?"

That's what Haley's mom had said, as Haley had slumped on the floor beside her bed, clutching the phone to her ear. "Couldn't we . . . you know . . . have some turkey?" Haley had asked plaintively.

Her mom had laughed. "Haley, sweetie, you know I can't fit a turkey in this fridge!" That was true. Her mom's tiny kitchen had a fridge the size of a shoebox, stuffed with chunks of cheeses with weird names, half-finished bottles of wine, and takeout containers. "Anyway, you should branch out. It's good for you. Honey, I'm having some friends over here for the dinner, you'll like them. Lucas has a show going up at the gallery next week and I showed him some of your photos. He was so impressed—"

"Mom!"

"What? I can't be proud of my own daughter?"

Be proud of me, sure, Haley had thought, squirming inside. *Just don't talk about me to people, okay?*

But her mom was already rattling on about the bus schedule and meeting Haley at Port Authority and how she was on no account to talk to anyone there, as if Haley hadn't done this a million times already since the divorce five years ago, and Haley was left thinking about the crisp brown skin of a turkey against the creamy white meat of the breast. Jewel-red cranberry sauce. Deep orange sweet potatoes with pale yellow butter melting into them. Haley saw it all arranged on a plate, the colors as harmonious as a still life. Perfect. Even if she didn't really like sweet potatoes and never ate the cranberry sauce.

Meanwhile, Jake had dealt himself one card and was waiting for Haley to say how many she wanted.

"It's fine," she said. "Um. Three cards. Ethiopian is fine. I mean, why not?"

Who was she to complain about eating unidentifiable food for Thanksgiving? Jake's fingers, as he rolled a red chip between them, looked as if they'd been whittled out of ivory. He was as thin as if he hadn't been eating anything at all.

"Bet, Haley, it's your bet. How's stuff at home?"

"Fine."

"Thank you for that detailed report."

Haley hesitated, looking over at the list Jake had written out for her. "Well, it's just. Fine," she said, talking to give herself time to think. "Eddie's getting into everything." Sticky hands and endless determination, that was Eddie. He had more powers of concentration than any two-year-old should really have. "But it's fine." She'd hoped for another jack to give herself three of a kind, but hadn't gotten it. Nothing but a pair. And Jake looked smug, gazing down at his hand. "I give up." She laid her cards facedown.

"Fold—you mean you fold. So everything's fine?" Jake turned his cards faceup as he raked the chips from the center of the table into his pile. He had two threes.

"You—I could have beaten you!"

"Too late now," Jake said calmly. "Next time we'll cover bluffing. Not that you really need a lesson in that. So do you get a cash bonus or something every time you use the word 'fine' in a sentence?"

"What?"

"It's fine if you're not fine all the time."

Haley blinked at her cousin. The one who'd shown her how to throw a punch in third grade when Adele Pinkney took Haley's new diary and the teacher had believed that it was

17

Adele's and not Haley's. The one who'd moved into her family's attic after his mom died, and who'd lived there for the last three years of high school. The one who'd given her her first good camera, a Canon SLR to replace her stupid Instamatic. She'd heard her father telling Jake he should have waited; it was way too expensive and complicated a camera for a ten-year-old. "She needs it," Jake had answered.

Even though she'd gone digital now, she kept the SLR on a shelf in her closet. Sometimes you needed the control a light meter gave you.

Haley looked at Jake, who, three months ago, had said he was done. Who'd quit with the blood tests and the new medications and the transfusions. Who'd said that if the doctors hadn't figured out what was wrong with his blood in twenty-three years, they weren't going to do it in the next six months.

Jake lifted one eyebrow, a dark angled streak against his pale skin. Haley reached into her pocket for her camera.

"No, I'm fine," Haley said after taking the picture. "I mean, everything's fine."

And it was true. Haley was fine. She wasn't the one who was dying.

"Okay. You're fine. Can you do something for me?"

"Sure."

He didn't have to ask. He knew—didn't he know?—that she'd do anything.

Sunny had put her head in Jake's lap again. Jake pulled at her ears gently. "Sunny—she's getting to be a little much for me. Even with you walking her every day. And the neighbors say she barks at night, sometimes. I don't know, I never hear her; maybe it's some other dog. But . . . " He didn't go on.

Haley felt an odd little shiver run through her stomach. Jake loved Sunny. He must be worse than she'd thought if he—

"You want me to take her?"

Jake didn't look down at the soft golden head in his lap, though his fingers kept mechanically scratching. "If your parents say it's all right. If they don't mind."

"No, they won't." Haley found she was standing up. Her feet were moving. She was walking backward toward the door of the apartment, and words were pouring out of her mouth, too quick, slippery. She couldn't stop them. "They won't mind. It's fine. Sure. I'll take her. And I'll bring her over to visit. All the time. You won't even miss her."

Jake smiled a little. "You should really ask them first, Haley."

"No, it's fine. I'm sure it's fine." Sunny's leash was hanging underneath Haley's coat. She snatched them both. "They won't mind. I'll take her with me. Don't—"

"Well, if they have a problem, bring her back. I'll find—"

"—worry. I'll take good care of her. You'll see. It's fine."

19

CHAPTER FOUR:
HALEY

Sunny had been puzzled but delighted when Haley had taken her leash down for a second time. Now she trotted happily alongside as Haley walked her bike down the sidewalk. But when they reached East Park, the dog stopped. The tiny playground was deserted now; empty swings rocked a little in the wind that had sprung up when the sun set. A rusty bolt chirped like a cicada, stranded in the wrong season.

When Haley tugged gently at the leash, Sunny braced her feet and whined.

"I know," Haley told her. "You don't understand. But it's different now." The wind was cold, a warning of winter; it stung tears from the corners of Haley's eyes. "Come on." She pulled at the leash again, and Sunny followed obediently. But at each corner, when Haley paused to let traffic go by, the dog looked back.

When they reached Haley's house, the kitchen windows were lit, warm yellow squares against the dark brick walls. You'd need a tripod to capture it, Haley thought. A handheld camera wouldn't stay still long enough to keep the focus sharp. It looked cozy and safe. In a photograph, it would say: home at the end of a long day. Comfort and peace.

Everybody thought photographs always told the truth. But a picture could be very deceiving.

Haley leaned her bike against the porch steps and led Sunny, her tail waving happily and her nose investigating every corner, up to the kitchen door. Haley pulled Sunny close and turned the knob.

Noise. That was the first thing that hit her. After the silence of the cemetery and the peace of Jake's apartment, it was like a slap, painful and shocking, no matter how much Haley had tried to brace herself for it. Elaine had given Eddie a big metal pot to play with, and he was whacking the bottom of it with both hands and shrieking happily. The radio was on loud, so Elaine could hear the news. Twelve people killed by a car bomb in Baghdad. Someone weeping. Sunny crowded nervously against Haley's leg.

"Haley, honey!" Elaine shouted. She was stirring a vat of spaghetti sauce on the stove. "Thank goodness! You can set the table. Your dad's going to be here any minute now and—what's that?"

Haley shut the door and dropped Sunny's leash as she stepped forward to block Eddie, who'd abandoned the pot and was making straight for the dog, both arms straight in front of him, fingers outstretched to grab. "It's Sunny," she said loudly as Eddie ran into her legs. Gunfire rattled from the radio. Haley raised her voice even more. "Jake asked me—"

Eddie tried to maneuver around the obstacle of his big sister. Haley grabbed his hands. Sunny gave a nervous little yelp.

"I *know* it's—" Stirring with one hand, Elaine reached over and switched off the radio with the other. "I know it's Sunny," she repeated. "What is Sunny doing *here*?"

"Jake asked me to—" Haley had to pick Eddie up and he yelled and kicked. Sunny, her leash trailing, made a dash for what looked like safety under the kitchen table. "To take her," Haley finished, grabbing Eddie more firmly around the waist. A determined two-year-old was harder to hold on to than a sack of angry cats. "He said he—ow! Eddie, *stop!*" For such a little kid, Eddie had quite a punch.

"Oh, here, give him to me." Elaine, tucking strands of her bright, coppery hair behind her ears, came over to take the struggling toddler. "Jake wanted you to take the dog? And you just—took her? Haley, why didn't you check with me or your dad?"

"I thought it would be okay." Eddie was really roaring now, arching his body back in Elaine's arms, his face growing red.

"Haley!" Elaine sounded mad too. "You can't just decide to bring a dog home. We don't even know if she'll be safe with Eddie."

"She's a good dog. She's *Jake's* dog!"

Haley stopped, appalled at the sound of her own voice. She sounded about five years old.

Elaine had heard too. She shifted Eddie to one arm and reached out a hand as if to put it on Haley's shoulder.

"Honey. I understand. But you have to think—"

"Fine," Haley interrupted, stepping back to avoid Elaine's hand. "We'll just drag her off to a shelter or something. Jake can't take care of her anymore, so we'll just put her to sleep. Then you'll be happy." As usual, the anger was helping. It patched up the crack in her voice, steadied her lips so they didn't tremble.

"Haley, that's not—" There was a frothing splash as the water boiled over on the stove. "Oh, just take her out of here! Take her up to your room for now. Then we'll talk."

Haley snatched up Sunny's leash. The dog was more than happy to be led out of the kitchen. Haley shut the door on Eddie's wails and Elaine's soothing voice.

Upstairs, she slid down to sit on the floor by her bed and hugged Sunny against her. The dog flopped down with her head in Haley's lap. Haley tugged at her ears, but Sunny didn't make the happy mooing noise she did when Jake petted her.

Haley knew she'd been unfair to Elaine. She didn't care. Jake wasn't Elaine's relative, after all. She hadn't even met him until she'd married Haley's dad three years ago.

Then a year after that there had been Eddie.

Nobody had asked Haley if she wanted a little brother. Wanted her sleep interrupted by crying, night after night. Wanted toys scattered all over her house and diapers stinking up the trash. Wanted every day to be scheduled around feeding Eddie and changing Eddie and getting Eddie to bed.

Of course, nobody had asked her if she wanted her parents to get divorced, either. Or her mom to move to New York. Or if she wanted a stepmother. Certainly nobody had asked her if she wanted her cousin to die.

Sunny pulled away from Haley's hands, shook herself so that the tags on her collar rattled, and went on a tour of inspection. She stuck her nose under piles of dirty clothes on the floor, checked out the bottom shelf of the bookcase, nudged a shabby teddy bear that leaned against a thick pile of photography books, and rooted under Haley's desk, where a snake's nest of dusty cables connected her computer and printer. Then Sunny pushed open the door to the closet, squeezed in, turned around twice, and flopped down on a pile of Haley's shoes.

The door to Haley's room swung open at the same time somebody tapped on it gently.

What's the point of knocking if you're going to open it anyway? Haley demanded silently. But she didn't say it, looking up at her father, leaning in the doorway. She was probably in enough trouble already.

Her dad came in and sat on the bed. "Where's Sunny?" he asked after a few moments.

Haley nodded at the closet. He leaned forward to peer inside.

"Ah. Well, if I were a dog in this house, I'd probably be looking for a safe place to hide too. You really should have asked first, Haley."

It was just a dog, after all. It was *Jake's* dog. It wasn't a slavering hellhound.

"I thought it would be fine," Haley said tightly. This time her voice didn't break.

"Hey. It's not that we don't *want* to keep her. If Jake asked—"

Haley, sitting on the floor, couldn't see her dad's face. But she could hear him stop and clear his throat. Haley felt her anger slip perilously. If her dad was nice to her now . . .

"Listen. We'll try it out. You'll have to help Eddie get used to Sunny. And if there's a problem—if it doesn't work, we'll find another home for her. Nobody's talking about taking Jake's dog to a shelter. All right?"

Haley stared fiercely at the doorknob on the closet door. If she blinked, she'd cry. She nodded. Once.

"Okay then. Dinner in five minutes. I expect you to apologize to Elaine when you come down."

That was it? That was all the trouble she was in for yelling at her stepmother and bringing a dog home without permission?

"And set the table. Every night. Until you go to college."

That was her job anyway. Haley looked up and managed a quick smile. Her dad put a heavy hand on her head and messed up her hair. His skin smelled of clay, dry and earthy and dusty.

"*Dad.* Now I'm going to have to comb it."

"Horrors. How's Jake doing?"

25

"Okay. Fine."

Her dad sighed. "Come on down to dinner, then. You better leave Sunny up here. What about *her* dinner? Did you get her food and stuff from Jake?"

"Um—"

"You didn't?"

"I brought her leash." Haley knew it sounded stupid. She hadn't even thought about Sunny's food, her bowls, the ratty plaid blanket she slept on.

"Never mind. We'll go to the pet store later. Get a few things."

He left. Haley brushed her hair. It was cut short, easy to take care of, and the dark red color sometimes made people think Elaine was her real mom. When she'd been younger— before Eddie was born—she'd kind of liked that. Now it irritated her.

Finished with her hair, she knelt down in front of the closet to give Sunny a hug. A warm, wet tongue swiped across her face.

"It'll be fine here," she whispered. "You'll see."

After dinner Haley brought Sunny downstairs. She knelt with one arm around the dog while her dad set Eddie down nearby. Elaine watched suspiciously.

Haley's dad caught Eddie when the little boy would have run at the dog. "Soft, Eddie," he cautioned sternly. "Be soft." He held Eddie's hand and stroked it gently down Sunny's flank. Sunny swiped her tail back and forth and sat panting with an air of bewilderment and cheerfulness. "Like that, Eddie, see? *Soft.*"

Her dad let go of the boy's hand and hovered over him, ready to snatch him back if necessary.

But Eddie didn't grab at Sunny's ears or poke at her eyes. He touched the soft golden fur of her side gently and then buried his hands in it up to his chubby wrists. Sunny turned her head to slather his hands with urgent licks. Eddie looked startled and then crowed with laughter. When he shrieked, Sunny jumped, but then transferred her attentions to his face, still sticky with the remains of tomato sauce from dinner.

Haley relaxed. "See? It's fine. She's fine."

Elaine came forward and bent down to pull Eddie away from his face bath. "That can't exactly be sanitary." But she was smiling.

The kid eats dirt, Haley wanted to say. *You think a few dog licks are going to matter?*

But instead she said, "Sorry." And it came out sounding all right. Not forced. Like she actually was.

"Oh, Haley, honey." Elaine smiled. "It's okay. It's fine."

Sunny, finding herself surrounded by faces at her level, distributed friendly licks all around. When Eddie grabbed at her tail she simply turned around to free herself and flopped down beside him. Eddie stamped his feet with happiness and petted her all over.

"Good girl, good girl." Elaine reached out to ruffle Sunny's ears. "She *is* gentle. What a sweetie."

Told you, Haley thought.

"Well, that's enough for her first night, I think." Haley's dad swept Eddie up, away from his fabulous moving, breathing, furry new toy. "Come on, little monster. Book? Story?"

"Down, down!" Eddie insisted.

"No down. Haley, take Sunny upstairs again. Let's do this gradually."

27

"Down down *down!*" Eddie bellowed. Elaine sighed. Haley gladly dragged Sunny upstairs and shut the door of her room on the noise. Sunny headed for the closet again. Haley took out her camera. Hooking it up to her laptop, she transferred the photos over and tapped the touchpad to move from one to the next, trying to make up her mind which to print out.

There, the close-up of Mercy's headstone. She zoomed in even closer, so that the letters, their edges softened by time and weather, filled the screen. She could almost make it an abstract, but the last sentence of the epitaph, down in the right-hand corner, still announced what it was—a life cut short.

Haley's thumb brushed the touchpad and a new photo flashed on the screen.

Jake had just glanced up at the camera. His skin, tinted a warm gold by the lamplight, almost gave him a look of health. But he'd grown so thin you could see the lines of his skull where it made hollows at his temples and under his cheekbones. Even his nose looked skinny. On the side away from the light, the shadows of the room curled around his face. One eye disappeared into them. His short black hair seemed to be dissolving into the darkness.

Haley slapped at a key to turn the program off, and Jake's face vanished from the screen.

CHAPTER FIVE:

HALEY

"**W**hy don't you go ask your aunt?" Haley's dad suggested, looking over her shoulder.

Haley had brought her prints of Mercy's grave and the cemetery down to the kitchen and spread them out on the table. The photos were the easy part. But she also had to write a report, and that was going to be a pain. The Browns may have lived in Rhode Island for a hundred years, but they'd never been the kind of people who made it into the history books. Where was Haley going to come up with enough details about Mercy's life to get an A?

She picked up a tangerine from the pottery bowl in the center of the table and looked up at her father. "Aunt Brown? She's your aunt, not my aunt." Digging her fingernails into the peel, she let loose a spray of sharp, sweet scent.

"Technically I think she may have been your grandfather's aunt. Except she was young enough to be his sister. Or something. I forget. The point is, she's got a bunch of family history stuff. Why don't you go out there and ask her? Maybe take Sunny with you. Elaine will have Eddie back from playgroup soon."

"Can you drive me?"

"Sorry, no can do, hon." Her father slathered peanut butter on a toasted bagel and took a bite, licking his fingers as he chewed. "Got a big order yesterday. Wedding present. Thank God people still get married."

That had always bugged Haley's mother, that her dad was happy to live on sales to the tourists in the summer and the occasional big order for a wedding. With his talent, he should be in museums, she said. Art galleries. Charging hundreds, maybe even a thousand, for a single piece. But her dad liked the idea of people *using* the pottery he made—coffee in his mugs, soup in his bowls, milk in his graceful pitchers with the long, slender necks.

"Could you take me to Aunt Brown's this afternoon, maybe?" Haley asked hopefully.

"Doubt it. What's wrong, got a flat tire on your bike?"

"No, it's—"

I just want you to come with me, Haley wanted to say. *Aunt Brown never acts like she likes me, and her house smells, you know it does . . .*

"She's kind of . . . " It was difficult to admit that your own aunt, or great-aunt, or great-great-aunt—could she be that old, really? No, her dad probably got it wrong, he was never good on details—that your own relative creeped you out.

And anyway, it would just be kind of nice if her dad did it because she'd asked. Mel's dad drove her to the mall any time she wanted.

"She's just kind of . . . weird," Haley finished lamely.

"She's hardly senile, Haley. I hope I'm in such good shape when I get to be her age."

"Well, she never leaves that house."

"She's eccentric. Every family should have an eccentric aunt. For atmosphere." Her dad stuffed the rest of his bagel into his mouth. "Good luck on the report. Home for lunch? I'll take a break from the studio and make us Reubens. Lots and lots of sauerkraut. How's that?"

He knew perfectly well that she hated sauerkraut. She threw the paper napkin at him. But she wasn't quick enough. The kitchen door closed behind him as he headed out to the studio he'd made of what had once been the garage.

Haley tried holding Sunny's leash in one hand and her bike's handlebars with the other. Sunny trotted happily alongside as Haley rode slowly away from town, out toward the country where there were fields with a few cows or maybe a horse.

Two more years and she'd have her license.

Aunt Brown lived at the top of a sloping hill, across the street from the cemetery Haley and Mel visited yesterday. *How's that for atmosphere?* Haley thought, leaning her bike against the mailbox. *Old farmhouse out in the country, graveyard right across the road.* All it needed was a thunderstorm and some ominous music.

Haley tugged at Sunny's leash and started up the long driveway, muddy and slippery, with only a few patches of gravel left. It would be scary to try to get a car up that, not to mention down. Of course, since Aunt Brown never went anywhere, getting a car in or out of her driveway wasn't really an issue.

The porch steps were worn and sagging. Paint had flaked off the walls of the house to show gray, weathered boards. Haley knew her dad had offered to come out and paint it one summer. But Aunt Brown liked it the way it was.

There was no doorbell. Haley knocked hard.

Sunny whined a little and pulled at her leash. "What, girl?" The dog was retreating away from the door, toward the porch steps.

"What? Is there a rabbit or something?" Sunny kept her eyes imploringly on Haley and dithered, her claws scrabbling at the floorboards.

"Why have you brought that animal here?"

Haley's heart jumped in her chest. She hadn't heard the door open.

Aunt Brown was standing in the doorway, looking disapproving. Of course, Haley couldn't imagine her looking any other way. She wore the same outfit she had worn every time Haley had seen her: the long skirt that nearly brushed the ground, the white blouse (how many did she have in her closet?), the silver locket about the size of a quarter that hung just under her collar, the cardigan that was faded to no true color at all, something between gray and blue and beige.

"Oh, hi. You startled me," she said a little weakly, petting Sunny, who pressed up close against her leg.

"Really? When I knock at a door, I generally expect somebody to open it."

"Oh. Yeah. Of course." Haley wanted to squirm. "I just—" She had to clear her throat. "Can I ask you a favor, Aunt Brown?"

"Leave the dog outside." Aunt Brown turned and walked inside, leaving the door open. Haley supposed that was meant as an invitation.

She looped Sunny's leash around the porch railing and rubbed the dog's ears reassuringly before she went in. Sunny let out a long yodeling yelp as Haley closed the door.

"Why did you bring that creature to my house?"

Haley's eyes were still adjusting to the change in light, and Aunt Brown's low, sharp voice seemed to come out of nowhere. "I didn't—" Haley blinked. She was standing in the hallway, the living room to one side, the dining room to the other. All the blinds were down, the air dim and gray. *Like living underwater,* she thought. The house was chilly. No wonder Aunt Brown always wore that cardigan. Haley kept her jacket on.

And there was that smell, one she recognized from her father's studio. Clay. It must come up from the basement. But it seemed to soak into the whole house, walls and ceilings, carpets and curtains.

"I didn't think you'd mind. She's Jake's dog." And that wasn't true, not anymore, but Haley knew she wouldn't stop saying it. "I'm just—keeping her."

"Don't bring her out here again. I don't like animals in the house." Now Haley could make Aunt Brown out, standing in the doorway to the dining room.

Sunny's not in the house, Haley thought rebelliously. But she said meekly, "I won't. I'm sorry."

Aunt Brown still looked displeased, as if an apology weren't enough. "Did you say you wanted something?"

To be gone was what Haley wanted now. Why didn't Aunt Brown ask Haley to come into the living room, or to sit down, or anything? Would it kill her to be friendly?

"I've just got this school project," she said awkwardly. "History. We're supposed to research an ancestor, you know? And I wanted to—you know, Mercy? Mercy Brown?"

It was strange how Aunt Brown just stood there, with those small, cool gray eyes fixed on Haley. Her eyelashes were so pale that she didn't seem to have any, and Haley couldn't see her blink. It was like being stared at by a snake.

"So I thought, Dad said, you might have some stuff about her?" Haley hated the way her voice was making everything she said into a question. "Family history stuff? That I could borrow?"

"Wait here."

Aunt Brown really didn't believe in wasting words. She just turned and left, her feet in their soft shoes silent on the old wooden floor.

Haley shivered a little. Didn't Aunt Brown notice how cold it was? She wandered into the dining room and twitched the curtains aside to look out the window. The sunlight that spilled into the room seemed faint and dishwater gray.

Restlessly, Haley moved around the room, brushing her hand over faded wallpaper, fingering carved wooden grapes and apples on a long sideboard. It was all slightly cold to the touch. Haley always had the feeling that everything in Aunt Brown's house should be covered with a light film of dust. She could almost see it, softening the carvings on the sideboard, dulling the shine of the pewter candlesticks on the table, clinging to the crystal of the chandelier. But there was no dust. Everything her fingers touched was perfectly clean. Haley imagined dust particles drifting in the air, too afraid of Aunt Brown to settle.

"Did you pull those curtains?"

For the second time in ten minutes, Haley jumped. Aunt Brown was just behind her.

Haley smiled nervously. She felt like an idiot. And it didn't help that Aunt Brown gave no answering smile, only stood looking sternly at her, as if Haley was expected to do something. In her hands was a bulky envelope, the brown paper soft with age and two of the corners split.

"The light will fade the furniture," Aunt Brown said.

Haley was baffled for a moment, then remembered the curtains. She hurried across the room to close them again.

Aunt Brown had set the envelope on the table and was carefully taking something out of it. A sheaf of papers, clipped together. An old newspaper, bits flaking off even as Aunt Brown laid it down. A small, flat box of cardboard that had once been red, tied shut with a yellow cord.

Haley came to the table to look at what her aunt had brought. Aunt Brown seemed interested as well. Having the elderly woman peer over her shoulder made Haley uncomfortable. She couldn't even hear her aunt breathing. She just—hovered.

But the historical stuff could be really useful. Haley bent over the newspaper first. She hadn't quite pulled the curtains together, she realized. A thin line of sunlight ran over the faded newsprint and touched the little box, laying a stripe of brighter red across its faded surface.

She looked at the opening paragraph of the newspaper article.

To begin with, we will say that our neighbor, a good and respectable citizen, George T. Brown, has been bereft of his wife and two grown-up daughters by consumption . . .

"This is from that time?" Haley said in surprise. "It was in the newspaper?"

"Certainly it was. Anything sensational is always of interest to fools."

Haley picked up one of the typewritten sheets next. It was a family tree. There was George Brown, and there was his wife Mary, and his daughter Grace, the other one who'd died, and little Edwin, and Mercy Lena.

"This is great." Haley looked up eagerly. "Aunt Brown, thanks. Can I take this stuff home? I'll be careful with it, I promise."

Aunt Brown's face was expressionless for a moment. Then she seemed to make up her mind.

"I suppose so. If you are responsible. You'll return it all, of course."

"Sure. I will. Of course." Haley made herself shut up. A simple "yes" would have done.

35

Aunt Brown had picked up the faded red box. Her fingers worried at the cord around it. "It's good to see someone taking an interest in history. The Browns are a very old family. Very old indeed. You ought to understand." She said the last sentence almost fiercely.

Haley found her attention riveted to the box in her aunt's hands. Her heart was beating a little quicker. As if she were expecting something wild, something dangerous, to pop out when Aunt Brown opened the lid. Stupid. She was being stupid. One of her hands had clenched tightly around the back of a chair, as if she needed support. Or protection, maybe?

Aunt Brown slipped the knot loose and opened the lid.

Inside was a glove. Leather that had once been soft and white was now yellow and stiff with age. The fingers had curled inward, as if an unseen hand inside the glove were trying to hold on to something.

"Can I see?" Haley reached out. "Was it Mercy's?" Aunt Brown nodded. All of Haley's earlier anxiety had vanished. She just wanted to hold the box, to touch Mercy's glove.

"It's fragile." Aunt Brown looked suspicious, as if Haley might grab hold of the glove and rip it to pieces. But she handed the box over, frowning. "You can't take that with you. It must be treated respectfully. But you may look at it."

Fascinated, Haley ran a finger gently along the glove's scalloped hem. The leather felt smooth and dry.

"The Browns are a very old family," Aunt Brown said again. Haley glanced up, but Aunt Brown didn't notice. She was looking so fixedly at Mercy's glove that Haley thought of a cat about to pounce on a mouse—hungry and excited and keyed up to a high pitch of eagerness.

"Can't I take it with me? It'll be great for my report. I promise, I'll be careful—"

"Certainly not. It's not something to be mauled about by a mob of schoolchildren. Give it to me."

Reluctantly, Haley handed the box back. Aunt Brown shut the lid and reached for the cord to tie it down. Frowning, she seemed to be thinking harder than such a simple task deserved.

Haley's fingers, deprived of the box, itched for her camera. She slid a hand into her jacket pocket. There it was. She'd tucked it in there before she left home, in case she came across an interesting shot.

Aunt Brown didn't notice Haley turning the camera on and holding it out, tipping it to get the right angle, to capture that look of concentration in her aunt's eyebrows, the tightness of her mouth.

Then Aunt Brown looked up. Haley's hand jerked just as her finger pressed the shutter.

"It is extremely rude to take a photograph without asking." Aunt Brown hadn't moved, but Haley found she'd shuffled backward a few steps. How could such a skinny little woman be so scary?

She found her voice. "I'm sorry. I didn't think . . . " She was so used to taking pictures of her family and friends—or rather, they were so used to her doing it—that she never hesitated. "I didn't mean to be rude."

"It is not a question of *meaning*," Aunt Brown said icily. "Manners are a matters of deeds, not intentions. I'm sure you have never been taught properly, but that is no excuse." She finished tying the cord as she spoke. Outside, there was a frantic barking and a scrabbling of claws on wood. Haley had left Sunny tied up for too long.

"You had better go, and take that animal with you." Aunt Brown slapped the box down sharply on the table. For all her talk about the glove being fragile, she wasn't taking such good care of it herself.

37

"Um. Sure. Thanks, Aunt Brown, really." Haley was shuffling the papers together, tucking them inside the old envelope. "I'll take care of this stuff, really."

"I'll expect it all back. In good condition."

"Of course. Sure. Of course." She was babbling. It was embarrassing. Outside, Sunny yelped. Aunt Brown took a step or two toward the hallway, as if she meant to do something about the noise the dog was making. Haley's hand reached out and her fingers closed around the red box.

By the time Aunt Brown looked back, Haley had stuffed the box inside the envelope with the papers. She hurried away from the table, hugging the envelope close so that Aunt Brown wouldn't notice its suspiciously lumpy condition. "Thanks." She forced herself to meet Aunt Brown's eyes and not to babble. "I'd better go. Sunny's getting upset." There. She could stop talking if she tried.

Aunt Brown walked her silently to the front door. The minute Haley was outside, Sunny flung herself at her, and Haley hurriedly knelt down to reassure her before the dog yanked the leash loose or scratched all the remaining paint off the porch floor.

Aunt Brown shut the door without a word of good-bye. *She must be scared of dogs,* Haley thought, and almost giggled. Aunt Brown, scared of Sunny? Sunny had to be the sappiest golden retriever around, and golden retrievers were not on anybody's list of vicious guard dogs anyway. Haley's imagination spun a quick giddy picture of Sunny standing guard at the airport or sniffing out bombs. If Sunny met a terrorist she'd probably lick him to death.

Now Sunny scrambled down the steps to the lawn, and Haley was dragged after her, clutching the envelope. The feel of the dusty dry paper between her fingers sobered her. Mercy's glove was in there. Why had she taken it? She didn't know. She hadn't thought about it. It had been just like taking a picture. With her camera on, she didn't think, *Ah, yes, that's the perfect composition, the lighting is ideal, the shadows just right.* She simply saw it through the lens, everything falling into place, the perfect shot assembling itself, and she pressed the shutter. *Click.* No thought required. As if her eye were wired directly to her finger.

It had been like that. That red box, sitting on the table with Mercy's glove inside. Her hand going out. *Click.*

Whatever the reason, she'd done it. She had the glove now. And she'd better get herself and Sunny out of the front yard before Aunt Brown noticed that the red box was missing.

CHAPTER SIX:
HALEY

The New England vampire tradition held little in common
with its counterparts and probable ancestors in Eastern
Europe.

Painfully, Haley dissected that sentence. New England
vampires weren't like the ones in Europe. No Draculas lurking
around the farmhouses and fields of Rhode Island. No capes and
Transylvanian accents. Right. She sighed and turned a page.

Indeed, the people who believed never used the term vampire
*themselves, though newspapers written by outsiders sometimes employed
it. The vampires of New England did not typically grow fangs, turn
into bats, or even crawl out of their graves. This curious legend, half
ghost story and half folk medicine, focused on the heart of a recently
deceased corpse, dead from the most dreaded disease of the time: tuberculosis. As long as fresh blood remained in that organ, legend said that the
corpse was in some way alive, surviving by sucking the life from its
nearest relatives—wives, husbands, brothers and sisters, children. As
entire families sickened and died of the disease, tales were whispered of
bodies disinterred by desperate relatives, who would find a fresh, red,*

41

*beating heart in the breast of a rotting corpse. To stake the heart or burn
it was the only remedy.*

Haley shuddered and flipped the book closed. Her New
England ancestors certainly had gruesome imaginations. It must
have been those long, dark, cold winters. Too much time to
dream this stuff up.

The box with Mercy's glove in it sat before her on her desk,
next to a few more library books, the envelope with Aunt
Brown's papers, and the laptop. Her father was off delivering
some of his pots to a gallery, and he'd taken Sunny with him;
she loved a ride in the car. Elaine was somewhere in the house,
doing laundry probably; with Eddie around there was a lot of
laundry. Haley thought she heard a low hum, like the dryer
running, and distant footsteps walking back and forth. Eddie had
to be asleep. Otherwise it would never be so quiet.

Haley flipped open a new book titled, invitingly, *The White
Plague*, and settled down to making notes. It didn't turn out to
be much more cheerful reading.

Tuberculosis (TB) / consumption
Symptoms—
    cough, pain w/ breathing
    weight loss
    fatigue
    chills
    loss of appetite
Transmitted by sneezing, coughing. But not easy to catch.
Need daily exposure, abt 6 months.

Mercy's mother and older sister had died of tuberculosis
before she did. She'd lived in the same house with them, taken
care of them. That must be how she'd gotten the disease. They

hadn't known, of course, back then, about germs, about infection, how sickness got transmitted.

But there had been other people in the house who hadn't gotten sick. Mercy's father had survived. Was it just luck, nothing more, that he'd lived and Mercy hadn't? Or had Mercy spent more time with the patients? The father, George, probably wouldn't have helped much. Nursing would have been women's work. Nothing he'd stoop to, even for his wife and daughters.

Haley laid her pen down.

Mercy must have known. When she began to cough up blood, to lose weight. She must have known she was going to die.

Haley's fingers were playing with the old yellow cord around the box that held Mercy's glove. One end was unraveling into threads, silky soft.

So who'd taken care of Mercy, then, when *she* was the one who got sick? If her mother and sister were already dead, if her father wouldn't have done it . . . Haley dug under a pile of books—this desk was too small, no room for all her stuff—and found the Brown family tree she'd made yesterday, copied from the one in Aunt Brown's papers. Yes. Grace hadn't been Mercy's only sister. There had been another one, Patience. The year of her birth was printed neatly under her name. She'd been five years older than Mercy. She must have been the one who nursed her little sister through tuberculosis.

Aunt Brown's family tree had been kept meticulously up to date. There was Haley herself, down in the right-hand corner, and there was Eddie, too, their birth dates neatly printed in small, precise handwriting. Idly Haley ran her finger along the branching lines that connected her to Mercy. Funny how much information you could get from names and dates. Look at this Brown, Elijah. His first wife had died and he'd remarried, but he'd already had three children. How had they liked their new stepmother? Mercy's father, George, had a sister and two broth-ers, so Mercy had an aunt and two uncles and—how many cousins? Haley went to count them up and her finger froze on the paper.

Oh, no. Look what she'd done. So *stupid*. Haley's eyes traveled back and forth between the family tree she'd written and the one Aunt Brown had lent her. Idiot. She'd skipped a whole generation. She'd linked up her great-grandfather directly with her great-great-great grandfather, who'd been Mercy's cousin James.

Now she'd have to do the whole thing over again. Haley crumpled up her family tree and threw it angrily at the wastebas-ket. What a waste of time. This whole stupid *project* was a waste of time, really. Look how long she'd been sitting here and she'd only managed to write down a third of a page on the symptoms of tuberculosis.

Suddenly Haley's backpack, on the floor next to her desk, blared out a bright tune. Haley jumped, tipping her chair back on two legs, before she recovered her balance and dug into the bag to find her phone under her math book. She glanced at the screen to see who was calling.

"Hey, Mel."

"Haley? You sound funny. Did you have to run for the phone?"

"Uh, no, I—" It was ridiculous, the way her heart was racing. "I was just—the phone startled me, I guess. What's up?"

"I'm in the car. We're going to the mall, Jen and Elissa and me—"

Haley could hear other voices. "Is she coming?" "Hey, I'm here too." "Do you girls have your seat belts on?" "*Yes*, Dad!"

"Shut up, I'm asking her. Haley? My dad says he can pick you up too. You want to come?"

On the one hand, she had to copy out the whole family tree again. And there was the algebra homework she hadn't even started. On the other hand, she hadn't been to the mall with Mel in—how long?

"Come *on*, Haley," Mel urged.

Haley smothered a little spasm of irritation. Mel *knew* she'd been busy lately, she *knew* what was going on—

—but still. The mall. A bright, normal, cheerful place, with stuff to eat and stuff to buy and lots of people and Mel and the other girls laughing and talking and sending texts back and forth to rate guys as they walked past—suddenly Haley wanted that, wanted it so much it hurt, a fierce grabbing pain in the back of her throat.

She had to cough and clear her throat before she said *yes* to Mel.

Then she stuffed the phone in her pocket as she ran downstairs. Her red jacket, her shoes. Where was her wallet? Oh, right, upstairs in her backpack. "Elaine?" Haley yelled. "I'm going to the mall. With Mel."

No answer. Her voice echoed lonesomely.

Haley opened the door to the basement and stuck her head in. "Elaine?" The light was off; no sound came from the washer or the dryer. Why had she thought Elaine was doing laundry?

She checked upstairs. No one in the bedrooms. And Eddie's crib was empty. The mobile above it, with tiny dogs in goggles and scarves flying little planes, twirled in a silent breeze.

Elaine must be out, and Eddie must be with her. Why had Haley been so sure her stepmother was in the house?

Back in her own room, Haley knelt to find her wallet in her backpack. When had it gotten so cold in here? Her arms, inside the sleeves of her jacket, had goose bumps. Her dad was so cheap with the heat. He hated to turn the furnace on before Thanksgiving.

There was her wallet, under her history book. She snagged it and stood up. The clutter on her desk tugged at her conscience a little. But it would just be for a few hours. There'd be plenty of time to work in the evening. She straightened up a few piles, stacked the books more neatly, put the lid back on the box that held Mercy's glove.

Hadn't that box been shut before? Haley looked down at it, puzzled. Her fingertips remembered the feel of the yellow cord. She'd been fiddling with it while she thought. She must have untied it without noticing.

It was so *quiet* in the house. So quiet and so cold. All at once Haley's spine prickled. She should go downstairs and watch for Mel's dad, but somehow she was very reluctant to leave her room. The skin at the back of her neck felt strangely vulnerable, as if someone was behind her. Someone might follow her along the hall, down the stairs . . .

A lock clicked. A door opened and shut.

"Haley!" It was Elaine's voice.

Haley's fears vanished. Reading all that stuff about sickness and death had creeped her out. That was all.

"Haley? Are you here? Come down and help me with the groceries."

Haley ran down the stairs. Elaine, pink-cheeked from the cold, had Eddie in one arm and a grocery bag in the other.

"Haley, thank goodness. There, get down, monster. Haley, honey, can you grab the groceries out of the car, please? Eddie, hold still, let me take off your coat. Well, stop wiggling and I'll be done faster."

Haley ran out to the driveway, snatched up two plastic grocery bags from the front seat, and ran back, dumping them on the kitchen counter. "Elaine, I'm—"

"Careful, that one has the eggs. Honey, I need a big favor— oh. You've got your coat on. You're going out?"

"To the mall. With Mel." Haley tucked her hands in the pockets of her jacket—she was still a little shivery—and felt her camera there.

"On a school night?"

"Elaine! It's not a school night. It's a school *day*. It's not even four o'clock. I'll be home for dinner."

"Haley. Wait a minute."

Haley paused. Elaine made an apologetic face.

"I'm sorry. Really. But I've got to show a house and I can't put it off. If I'd known you had plans . . . "

"You need me to babysit." Haley didn't even have to make it a question.

"I'm so sorry." Elaine was smoothing her hair, checking her lipstick in the mirror by the door, grabbing her briefcase from the counter. "This just came up at the last minute, and your dad won't be home from making his deliveries until six. I'm sorry, sweetie, I *can't* neglect this client. If I don't sell somebody a house soon, we'll be eating oatmeal for supper. Just make him a scrambled egg, order a pizza for you and your dad if you want. Maybe Mel can come over after the mall? Bye, thanks, you're a hero, I'm so sorry about this—" The door shut behind her.

Eddie stared at the door in outrage. "Mama!" he bellowed.

"Oh, great." Haley sighed.

Not bothering to take off her jacket, she bent over to pick Eddie up. His scream nearly ruptured her eardrum. "Hey, Eddie, hey, listen, it's okay. Mama's coming back. Hey, don't cry, shhh, shhhh . . . " She tried to jiggle Eddie up and down—sometimes that worked—but his body was rigid and he was arching back in her arms, yelling.

"Okay, fine." Haley carried him into the living room and dumped him on the soft carpet, where he could kick and thrash if he wanted to without hurting himself. "Go ahead, cry. Like it's

47

such a tragedy being stuck here with me. This wasn't my idea of fun either," she informed the little boy.

Eddie howled. There were no tears, Haley noticed. It was pure rage. His world had been disrupted, his plans had been laid aside, and it was all simply unacceptable.

"Yeah, well, welcome to the world, kid," Haley muttered, and flopped down on the couch. When Eddie got like this there was no solution but to let him cry it out. In a few minutes he'd calm down a little and she'd get him a cookie, which would bring a good mood back like flipping a switch. Then she'd call Mel and cancel when there wouldn't be screaming in the background. Elaine didn't approve of her bribing Eddie with food, but Elaine wasn't around, was she?

Haley felt the camera in her pocket nudge against her side and took it out. Turning it on, she focused on Eddie, zooming in for a close-up. His face was as red as a brick, his eyes squinched tight shut, his mouth open as wide as it could go. She clicked the shutter, zoomed in even more. Her brother's angry face filled the screen the way his screams filled the room.

CHAPTER SEVEN:
MERCY

I t was the heart of winter. Too cold to dig a grave.

In the churchyard there was a crypt aboveground, built of stones from the field. We were not a wealthy congregation and had no money to spare on fancy stonework for the dead. This was where they laid my body to wait until the ground thawed.

My father, by that time, had been wrung dry of tears. He stood watching as they slid my coffin into its resting place. Huddled in his long brown woolen coat, the collar turned up to his ears, the beard that he kept thick and long in winter covering half his face, he looked baffled and angry, not grief-stricken. Like a great bear woken too early from his winter sleep. He looked as if he wanted to roar with fury, swing a strong clawed arm and split someone in two. But who was there for him to attack? Where could his rage go?

Behind my father, a little to one side, were his two remaining children. Patience had Edwin by the hand. All around her, people tugged capes and coats closer, hugged their arms tight, but Patience was never bothered by the cold. She looked as if she were counting the mourners, adding up the total in her mind, calculating the respect shown to the Brown family.

Some of the women wept openly. The men frowned and shuffled their feet. None of them gathered together to whisper, to cast sidelong glances, to put fear into ugly shapes, into words with claws and fangs to hurt, words with wings to flit from ear to ear, mind to mind, heart to heart.

That would come later.

Edwin clung to Patience's hand. Thin and pale, he looked half-smothered in coat and scarf and cap. He shivered in the icy air.

CHAPTER EIGHT:
HALEY

Sunny was so happy to see Jake that she couldn't contain herself. She wouldn't jump on him, but she nearly crawled up onto his lap as he sat on the edge of his bed. After letting him pet her for a few seconds, she flung herself away to race around the room, sniffing eagerly at everything her nose could reach, before returning to Jake's side, panting happily.

Maia laughed. "Now I see what I've been doing wrong. All those dates I've been on—what a waste! I need to get myself a dog. Just someone to be that glad to see me when I get home."

Jake still had his pajamas on, a limp gray T-shirt over flannel pants, his feet bare. That meant he probably hadn't gotten out of bed until Maia had arrived. He hadn't shaved.

"Much, much better than dating," Jake agreed, fondling Sunny's ears. "For one thing, it's not so expensive to take her out to dinner."

Maia's laugh was rich and dark and chocolaty. Haley had never understood how Maia could be so happy. A visiting nurse for terminal patients, spending her days with dying people— how was this a cheerful job?

Maia was checking Jake's medications, seeing if he needed refills. "You taking these new ones?" She waved a tiny brown bottle at Jake.

"Sometimes."

"They don't do you any good in the bottle, you know."

"I take them when I need them. Don't fuss."

"Well, fussing. Lord forbid I should fuss. Haley, you gorgeous thing, how's school treating you? Beating those boys off with a stick?"

Haley used to blush and squirm when Maia teased. Now she hung up her jacket and shrugged. "A great big one. With nails in it."

"I'm getting her karate lessons for her birthday," Jake added. "That's the only thing that will keep the guys at bay."

While Maia laughed some more, Haley wandered around the room. She took a mug stained with coffee dregs to the kitchen and rinsed it out. She picked up a book, a fat paperback mystery, lying facedown on the arm of Jake's chair, and dog-eared the page, closing it neatly, smoothing the creased spine.

"You have another nosebleed last night?" Maia asked. Haley, glancing up, saw Maia frowning at the rusty brown stains on Jake's pillowcase.

Jake's voice was uninterested. "Apparently."

A sketchbook was lying on the table. Jake had been drawing something. A crumbling stone wall with a wide arched opening. The shadows inside the arch were thick and black. He'd pressed hard enough on the pencil to dent the paper and scatter little grains of carbon across the page. Haley blew them gently away. In the corner of the page, Jake had scrawled, *Macbeth*.

Haley stacked the sketchbook and the mystery novel on the table, lining up the edges precisely. She collected two pencils and a stick of charcoal and laid them neatly alongside. All this let her keep her head down as Maia checked Jake's blood pressure. She didn't like to see her cousin's arm as Maia wrapped the cuff around it, to notice how thin it had gotten, the bicep no thicker than his forearm.

Maia let out her breath in a *hmmph* sound as she looked at the numbers on her dial and whipped the cuff off Jake's arm. "Let's get you on a scale, then. Come on, I haven't got all day."

"Oh, you're the one with the hot date tonight?" Jake got to his feet. Out of the corner of her eye, Haley saw him wobble a little. Maia's hand moved quickly to his elbow to steady him.

The scale creaked a little as Jake stepped onto it. Maia went *hmmph* again.

"You drinking those milkshakes I brought?"

A bright thread glinted on the floor, near a leg of Jake's chair. Haley bent down for it.

"The ones that taste like cardboard? Yes." Jake's voice sounded as if he'd been running hard rather than walking a few feet.

The thread came up in Haley's fingers. It was actually a chain of small silver links. The clasp on one end was broken.

Slow footsteps, dragging a little, and Sunny's claws clicking on the wooden floor. Jake sank into his chair beside Haley. Sunny laid her head on his lap, and the hand he lifted to stroke her ears trembled very slightly.

Shifting her eyes quickly from his face, Haley held the chain out to Maia, glad for the excuse to talk about something that wasn't Jake's health. "Is this yours?"

"Why would I wear a thing like that?" Maia shook her head a little so that her earrings—dangling confections of jade and ivory and something purple—swung and chimed quietly. "That's something my grandmother would wear."

"Well, then, whose is it?"

"Maybe it's Elaine's." Jake glanced briefly at the necklace. "She and your dad were here a couple of days ago. Maybe she dropped it."

"Elaine doesn't wear jewelry. She says you can have jewelry or a child under three, but not both."

"Must be somebody else's, then." Jake leaned his head against the back of the chair.

"Haley, come on in the kitchen," Maia told her. "I'm going to make myself a cup of tea, since your cousin there's too lazy to act like a host."

Haley slipped the necklace into her pocket as she followed Maia. The nurse filled a kettle and set it on the stove. "Get down some mugs, will you?" She snorted as she pulled open a cupboard. "I'm going to bring that man some real tea. Nothing here but this pomegranate stuff. It'll have to do, I guess."

Maia dumped tea bags into Jake's mugs. Earth brown with splashes of green like pine trees, and Haley's father's initials—NJB, for Nathan Joseph Brown—scribbled onto the bottom. Steaming water poured over the tea bags.

"Haley. Honey," Maia said softly. "You can see it, right?"

Haley picked up her tea, curling her hands around the hot mug. "See what?"

"He's getting worse."

Haley froze, holding her mug to her lips, looking at Maia through the steam. "But—but, that new medicine—you told him he should take it. Won't that help?"

"That's just to help with the nightmares, baby. So he can get some sleep. It's not going to cure him."

The thin layer of clay between Haley's hands and the scalding water was growing hotter and hotter. In a minute she'd have to put the cup down.

"But—but there's something, right? That you can do?" She remembered to keep her voice low. "Something more that he can try. Something—"

"He doesn't want to try anything new, Haley." Pity softened Maia's voice. One corner of her wide mouth tucked in a little, as if to control her own pain. "You know that, honey. You knew it when he came home from the hospital this last time."

"But not—but not so *soon!*" Hot water sloshed over the edge of Haley's mug and onto her fingers. It hurt. "Six months. He said six months. The doctor said—"

Six months. That was half a year.

"That wasn't a guarantee, honey. It was just a guess."

Doctors weren't supposed to guess. They were supposed to *know*.

And they'd said six months. Back in August, they'd said six months. Not until winter, they'd said. And it was only November.

Six months was half a year.

The first snow hadn't even fallen yet.

Six months was still a long time away.

And now Mercy's glove was missing.

Haley's report was due tomorrow. She'd finished her display and printed out her notes. Now she was packing up the papers Aunt Brown had given her. She slid the newspaper article and the family tree back in their envelope and laid the package on her bed. But where was the red box with Mercy's glove?

Nothing, *nothing*, stayed where it was supposed to in this house. Haley went back to her desk, picked up books and looked beneath them, checked behind the printer and the laptop. She got down on her hands and knees to look underneath. Nothing but dust and cables.

This was crazy. Haley had left the box on the desk. She *remembered*. Could her dad have taken it? Or Elaine? Why would they?

"Mine, mine!" Eddie said, delighted. Haley scrambled to her feet and snatched the envelope full of Aunt Brown's papers out of Eddie's hands.

"Mine!" he insisted angrily.

"*Not* yours," Haley objected. "No, Eddie, leave that alone!" He'd grabbed a fat blue pillow off her bed this time. It had a photo printed on it, Haley at six, grinning a wide, gap-toothed smile, hugged between her parents.

That had been eight years ago. More than half her lifetime. Eight years; that was a long time. Next to eight years, six months looked like—

"Give it back," Haley told Eddie.

Giggling, thrilled to have her attention, Eddie ran out of the room and thumped into Elaine, a basket of clean laundry balanced on her hip.

"It's not a game!" Haley yelled after him. "Elaine, that's my pillow. Get it away from him. He'll spill something on it."

"He's not going to hurt it, Haley." Elaine set the laundry basket down with a tired sigh. But she bribed Eddie to give up the pillow, handing over a pair of rolled-up socks in exchange.

"You don't know what he's going to do," Haley grumbled. "And Mercy's glove is missing. If he took it—"

"Who? Eddie?" Elaine looked up, startled. "What would he want with an old glove?"

"What does he want with anything? What did he want with my flash drive last week?"

"Well, you shouldn't have left it on the coffee table."

Of course it had been Haley's own fault that Eddie had dunked Haley's drive in Sunny's water dish. She couldn't even leave something on the coffee table in her own house.

"And we said we'd replace the drive. Honestly, Haley . . . "

"How are you going to replace an antique glove? A historical one? A, a, an *heirloom?" An heirloom you weren't supposed to take,* Haley's conscience whispered, and her stomach squirmed. If she had to tell Aunt Brown that she'd taken the glove and Eddie had ripped it up or chewed on it or fed it to Sunny . . . Her imagination cringed.

"Haley." Elaine's lips tightened. "Why don't we look for it first? Before we try, convict, and execute Eddie for taking it?"

"*I'll* look for it," Haley snapped. "Just—can't you keep him out of my room?"

"Not if you leave the door open." Elaine picked up a folded shirt and three pairs of socks out of the laundry basket and handed them to Haley. "Here. If you want me to wash that stuff on the floor, you know you've got to get it in the laundry basket. And what's that on your bed? Isn't that what you're looking for?"

She heaved the basket back up and followed Eddie down the hall. Haley looked back over her shoulder. The red box was lying on her quilt, open. The fingers of the glove spilled over the edge, pale against Haley's dark blue quilt.

She couldn't have missed seeing it, if it had been there before.

Except she must have. What was she imagining? That the box had moved by itself? That the glove had crawled out while her back was turned?

Now there was a creepy thought. Creepy but stupid. She just hadn't seen the box, somehow. Hadn't seen a red box on a blue quilt.

The glove *did* look a bit as though it had tried to crawl out of the box on its own, though. Haley fought back a shudder at the thought of those flat white fingers stirring to life, like blind white worms.

She reached out a hand to put the glove back into the box and then stopped.

Eddie *had* done something to it! There were stains all over the ivory leather, rusty splotches, brown tinged with red. Appalled, Haley snatched the glove up. Was it peanut butter? No, the marks were a deeper red than that. And so fresh they glistened, shiny and wet. So fresh they were spreading, getting larger and larger, meeting and merging into one large gory stain the color of blood.

Haley dropped the glove on her bed. Now the stuff—whatever it was—would be all over her quilt. But it was on her hands too—gross! Haley rushed for the bathroom, turned the hot water on hard, and stuck her hands under the stream. Faintly pink water swirled down the drain.

Hands clean again, she came back to her room. What was she going to do? There was no way, just no way, she could tell Aunt Brown. Maybe she could lie. Maybe she could bury the thing in the backyard. Maybe she could clean it somehow.

She picked the glove up gingerly, by one finger. It felt warm against her skin, almost as if it had just been pulled off of a living hand.

And it was clean. Nothing on the pale leather but the yellow tinge of age.

Haley turned the glove over and over, staring at it. It was spotless.

A trick of the light, maybe. Her eyes had fooled her.

But if that was true, what had she just washed off her hands?

Carefully, Haley packed the glove away. She wrapped the yellow cord several times around the box and tied the knot tight.

CHAPTER NINE:
HALEY

"**I**f untreated, tuberculosis, or consumption, which is what people called it back then, had a death rate of fifty percent. It, um, it had killed two people in the Brown family before Mercy." Haley stopped to clear her throat. "It was, it was . . ." She glanced hurriedly down at her notes. "It was sad. It was tragic. But it wasn't supernatural or anything." *Or anything, great, Haley, that sounds really sophisticated.* From the back of the room, Mr. Samuelson gave her a quick smile and nodded encouragingly, which only rattled her further. If he thought she needed encouragement, she must be doing badly.

"Not everyone at the time believed in this old New England superstition. Not even everybody in Mercy's family did. Umm . . ." Her eyes skittered down over her notes, found the right place. "A reporter wrote an article for a newspaper right after it happened. This is what he said. 'The husband and father of the deceased has, from the first, disclaimed any faith in the vampire theory, but being urged, he allowed other, if not wiser, counsel to prevail.' " Thank goodness for Aunt Brown's newspaper. It really made her report sound historical.

"Everybody was looking for somebody to blame, and they picked Mercy. It was like a trial by mob. Only Mercy didn't really get to defend herself. Since she was, um, dead." The few people who were listening laughed. "Superstition and ignorance made a natural tragedy into something worse," Haley said in a rush, then gathered up her notes and sat down so they'd all stop looking at her.

Mr. Samuelson led the brief round of applause. "Very colorful, Haley, thank you. All right—that's the last report for today. Chelsea, you're up first tomorrow. Remember, by the end of the week you should be finished with chapter eleven and—" The bell rang, cutting off his words.

Haley shoveled her laptop and her notes into her backpack. Mel leaned over her desk. "Haley, that was really good."

"I got nervous." Haley made a face.

"I couldn't tell."

Haley knew Mel was just being nice, but wasn't that what best friends did? She grinned, comforted, as she got up. It was too bad every school project seemed to involve writing something. Reports definitely weren't her best area. But if she could just get graded on the display . . .

Haley looked up at her poster board. Her captions, maybe, were brief compared to some of the others ranged along the blackboard. Annie Lewis's display was almost completely covered in pages of neatly typed text. But what did you need words for when that photo of Mercy's gravestone was in the center? Dead at nineteen. Dead, demonized, blamed for something she could never have done. A victim of ugly superstition as much as of a fatal disease.

"I vant to suck your bloooood," moaned a voice in Haley's ear. She jumped. Papers and pens spilled out of her open backpack to the floor and her laptop nearly followed.

"Knock it off, Jaffe."

Thomas Jaffe laughed ghoulishly and widened his eyes. "Hey, Lady Dracula, want to bite me? I'll show you where—"

"Shut up, Thomas, you're disgusting." Mel glared at him, hugging her books tighter over her chest. As Haley bent over to pick up her belongings, Thomas closed his hands lightly around her neck from behind.

"Get off!" Standing up quickly, Haley jammed her elbow back into Thomas's ribs.

"Hey, ow!" Thomas let go. "I was just kidding!"

"You were just stupid," Haley snapped.

"Check her out, she's scary."

"Watch out, biting might run in the family."

"Maybe she wants to bite *all* of us . . ."

Haley felt her stomach tighten. She clutched her backpack closer. Even though it was just Thomas and his friends, Andy Chen and Kevin Christianson, acting like idiots as usual. What was she so tense about? What could they possibly do to her in the middle of a brightly lit classroom, with Mr. Samuelson right outside the door, yelling at some kid to stop running in the hall?

"Come on, Haley." Mel's voice dripped disdain. "Let's go."

But Thomas blocked Haley's path, rubbing his ribs. She glared. He didn't move.

"Haley, you dropped this."

The voice was quiet. Haley turned to look at Alan O'Neil, holding out a page of her notes. She hadn't even heard him come up behind her.

"That was really interesting," he said calmly, and eased past Haley in the narrow aisle between the desks. Pausing, he waited for Thomas to move. He looked as if the possibility of Thomas doing anything else had never crossed his mind.

Thomas fell back a few paces and turned, heading for the door. Andy and Kevin followed.

Haley felt ridiculously relieved, almost shaky. "Thanks."

"For what?" Alan looked back. "Picking up your notes?"

"Yeah." Haley tried to remember if she'd ever talked to Alan O'Neil before, beyond "Excuse me," and "What chapter are we supposed to read?" Didn't he play basketball? Or hockey? Or something? She couldn't imagine why he'd come to her rescue, but she thought she was even more grateful to him for pretending there'd been nothing to rescue her from than for making Thomas Jaffe back off. "Yeah, for picking up my notes. Thanks."

"No problem."

She expected Alan to drift off once they reached the hallway and she caught up with Mel, but somehow the three of them stayed together into the cafeteria and through the line past pizza, chicken sandwiches, and the salad bar. Haley, her slice of pepperoni cooling on her plate, flicked quick glances at Alan's face after they'd all found seats at one of the little round tables. He'd photograph well, that fair skin against the black of his eyes and eyebrows and shaggy, loose hair. All that contrast. Alan and Mel were talking about Lucy Williams's great-great-grandmother, who'd survived the *Titanic*. Haley's fingers itched for her camera.

"Haley, what do you think? The Chicago fire or the San Francisco earthquake?"

"What?"

Mel rolled her eyes. "What disaster would you rather have an ancestor live through?"

"I don't—I don't know. As long as they live, who cares?"

"The practical approach," Alan said thoughtfully. He disdainfully removed the lettuce from his sandwich. "Efficient, but a little lacking in nuance."

"So if you're not paying the least bit of attention to what we're saying," Mel inquired, poking around for the bits of ham in her salad, "what are you spending your lunchtime thinking about?"

"Mercy, I guess." Which was better than saying out loud that she'd been thinking about the dark lines of Alan's eyebrows and the way his jaw moved when he chewed.

Mel sighed. "Haley, your project's done. You definitely got an A. Relax, can't you?"

Haley looked down, surprised to find half of her pizza gone. She didn't remember taking a bite. "I know. It's just . . . it's just . . . I don't get it, really."

"Get what?" Mel asked patiently.

"How people could do that. I mean, they *knew* her. Exeter was a really small town back then." Haley hadn't actually been thinking about this, but now that she'd started talking, it was as if it had been in her mind all along. "We're talking about people who knew her when she was a little girl, people she went to school with. Her *family*. How could they have thought she was evil?" Actually evil, like some monster out of a horror movie. Fresh, warm blood in her dead, cold heart.

Haley blinked hard to get that image out of her brain and went on talking. "How could her *father* have thought so?"

"Well, he didn't think so," Mel pointed out. "You said. Other people talked him into it."

"But he let them. He agreed. How could anybody do that?"

Blood so wet and fresh that it glistened. Like those red stains on Mercy's glove.

"That's easy. Fear."

Haley looked over at Alan. He shrugged and took a huge bite of his sandwich.

"You said it all yourself, Haley." He swallowed. "Tuberculosis had a fifty percent death rate. There were, what, six people in Mercy's family? And four of them died?" He really had been paying attention to her report. Haley was surprised. She'd assumed that most people, except for Mr. Samuelson (who got paid to listen) had been dozing or daydreaming or thinking about their own reports. "People were scared," Alan went on. "You can't blame them, really. When people get scared, they just get stupid. And they look around for somebody to blame."

"That's no excuse," Haley snapped. She looked down at her plate, smeared with greasy red tomato sauce, and her stomach heaved. She had to swallow hard. "I don't care how scared they were. Her father could have stuck to reason, at least. If he'd loved her at all, he would have."

"He was worried about his son, though," Mel pointed out, looking at Haley a little oddly. "What was his name—Edwin? Hey, is Eddie named after him?"

"Eddie's Edward. He's named after Elaine's dad." Haley peeled clingy plastic wrap away from a brownie, hoping a bite of that would get the sour taste out of her mouth. "All that proves is that Mercy's dad loved Edwin more than her. Typical. For that time. Loving the son more."

"The son was still alive," Alan said quietly. "I mean, Mercy was already—Haley? You okay?"

Haley dropped the brownie on the table.

"If you really love somebody, you don't stop just because they're dead," she said coldly. She got to her feet, snatched up her tray, and went to dump the rest of her lunch in the trash.

Suddenly she hated school. Hated the bright, loud cafeteria, hated the talking and laughing and shouting that battered at her ears. Hated the smells of steamed food and salt and grease. Hated the hallways with their shiny linoleum, full of jerks like Thomas Jaffe, full of people like Mel and now, maybe, Alan who were supposed to be her friends but who just didn't get it. They didn't even get that there was something they couldn't understand.

So she did something she had never done in all of her years at school. She walked out.

It was ridiculous, how easy it was. She just went to her locker, stuffed her laptop and a few books into her backpack, grabbed her jacket, and left by the front door. Nobody stopped her. Nobody asked where she was going. Maybe they thought she was sick, or assumed she had a doctor's appointment. Maybe they just didn't care.

Haley set off quickly down the street. She wanted to see the one person she could count on to understand death and dying.

CHAPTER TEN:
HALEY

J ake, stretched out with a book in his armchair, glanced at the clock when Haley opened his door. But that was all. He must have known she was cutting class, but he didn't say a word about the time.

"You brought your laptop?" he asked, eyeing her backpack. "You got some new photos to show me?"

The tightness inside Haley's chest eased a little. And she felt herself relaxing more when she took a second look at her cousin. Jake looked better. His voice was firmer. His eyes were alert.

Haley grinned to herself as she flipped open her computer and turned it on. Maia meant well, but she wasn't a doctor. She didn't know everything. Setting the laptop on the table by Jake's chair, she nudged aside the black ashtray. It had a half-smoked cigarette in it. Liam must have been by to visit, even though it wasn't Saturday. Haley turned off the tall floor lamp so nothing would reflect off the screen.

"See, those are the ones for my history project. The gravestone and the cemetery . . ." She tilted the laptop so that Jake could see and tapped the touchpad to move through the images.

"That's good. The one with the tree leaning toward the grave. And the black-and-white. Strong. Go back, I want to see that one of the stone wall again."

Most people—even Mel, even her dad and Elaine—flipped through photos like the goal was to get to the end as quickly as possible. Jake really looked.

A stray thought flickered into her mind. Alan O'Neil, now. Would he really look?

The thought of Alan brought her mind back to the lunch she'd walked out on, and the tomato sauce on her plate. Sticky and red, like half-dried blood.

And that made her think of the stains on Mercy's glove.

She glanced quickly up at Jake's face as he stared at the screen. Would he laugh if she told him how creeped out she'd been?

No, of course not. Jake had never laughed at her.

"Listen," she said.

"What?" Jake dug into his shirt pocket for a book of matches, picked up the half-smoked cigarette from the ashtray, lit it, and put it to his lips. The tip glowed as he breathed in, a spot of vivid orange.

Haley stared at him in shock. "What are you doing?"

Jake blew white smoke gently at the computer screen. It swirled and drifted like eddies in a quiet stream. "Nice. I like how the line of the stone wall moves to that upper corner. What were you going to say?"

"You're *smoking*!"

"Well—yeah." Jake looked down at the cigarette between his fingers. "I used to, a little, in college. It was hanging out with all those theater majors. Half of them smoke, I don't know why. You'd think they'd want to take care of their voices. I guess it's a weight thing—"

"You can't *smoke*!" Haley was outraged.

"Why not?" Without moving his head, Jake lifted his eyes to her face.

"*Because*. Because it will—"

Jake waited, quietly, for her to finish. She couldn't.

"It's gross. It's disgusting," she said at last, fighting the urge to snatch the cigarette out of Jake's hand and grind it to ash beneath her shoe. "It's—and what about secondhand smoke?" she demanded triumphantly. "You think I want to breathe that every time I come over?"

"Okay," Jake said mildly. He put the cigarette out in the ashtray. "I won't smoke when you're here. You could open the window, if it bothers you."

If it *bothered* her! Haley felt as if an electric shock had hit her right on top of her head. Its energy sizzled along her nerves. She wanted to jump up, yell, run, hit something as hard as she could. How could Jake just sit there calmly, like it was no big deal?

"Come on, Haley. It's not like it's going to kill me."

After the heat of the electric shock, icy cold. "Don't do that," Haley said.

"Do what?"

"Make jokes." Her voice still rasped, as if the smoke from the cigarette had already corroded her vocal cords. "Like you don't care."

"I'm the one who's dying, Haley." He could have said it impatiently. But there was sympathy in his face, gentleness in his voice. Too much. Haley felt her throat closing up with that old, sharp pain that meant tears would be on the way soon if she didn't change the subject quickly. "I pretty much have to care. I'm just . . ." He put a hand out and flicked his fingers into the air, as if brushing something insubstantial away. "Not going to cry about it every minute. What do you expect me to do?"

"Try."

She whispered it. Jake frowned and leaned forward a little, as if he hadn't quite heard her.

Haley leaned forward too, her hands on her knees. Her heart began to beat a little quicker. "You could, you could talk to the doctors some more. You could—" Jake was shaking his head. Haley's fingers were pinching her knees tightly. She'd have bruises in the morning. Right now she hardly noticed. "There might be something you could do!" Jake looked as if he felt sorry for her, and the idea put an edge in her voice, made it louder. He shouldn't feel sorry for her, he should *listen* to her; she was *right.* "If you went back to the hospital, tried some new stuff, if you just *tried*—"

"I did try. I tried for a long time. Now I'm done."

Haley froze. She couldn't move. Except for her heart, which still beat out a frantically quick tattoo against her ribs.

"I'm sorry. Really. To put you through all this. But—you remember my mom, Haley? You remember how she died?"

Aunt Nell's face on the hospital pillow. Her lips and eyelids an ashy blue. Her skin as pale as her wispy, white-blonde hair.

"For a year, all we talked about was her health. Or lack thereof. The last year of my mom's life, all we talked about was tests and medicine and how many milligrams of this and how many milligrams of that. For a *year.* The last thing I said to her was, 'The next transfusion's at eight-thirty tomorrow.' That's the last thing I said to my mother. I just don't want to do that again."

He picked up the unlit cigarette and tapped it restlessly on the edge of the ashtray.

"You can get as mad as you want," he told Haley. "But remember, when you're done being angry, I'll still be dying."

Haley didn't talk much for the rest of the day. Somehow she felt as if she needed to keep everything quiet. As if there was an unexploded bomb inside her and any loud sound, any sudden movement, would set off the explosion.

The bomb had started ticking with Jake's words. *I'll still be dying.*

She stayed silent all through dinner. Nobody could carry on a conversation at the table anyway. Not with Eddie trying as hard as he could to wear most of his food as body art.

She headed up to her room after the meal was over, her feet in thick socks noiseless on the stairs. She was so quiet that Elaine and her father, still in the dining room, didn't hear her.

But she could hear them.

" . . . really don't know what do with her." Elaine was speaking. "Half the time she doesn't say a word, or she's so mad at Eddie . . . treats me like the evil stepmother . . ."

And then her dad's voice, heavy and resigned. "I'll talk to her."

So now she was a problem to be talked to, was she? Well, he couldn't talk to her if she wasn't in the house. Haley backed up quietly. Kitchen, back door. Shoes, where were her shoes? Elaine's pumps and her running shoes, Dad's clay-splattered work boots, Eddie's tiny sneakers. There were so many shoes here, nobody could ever find anything. All this clutter, all over the house; no wonder all her stuff got lost—shoes, gloves, *everything*. Everything she ever cared about vanished.

At last Haley found her sneakers and was bent over, lacing them up, when her dad came into the hallway, bringing the earthy scent of clay with him, buried deep in the threads of his old corduroy shirt, once green, now gray. He'd washed up at the studio but he'd missed the smudge of clay that had dried in his left eyebrow.

"Taking Sunny out?"

Haley nodded. Her throat ached fiercely. She yanked a shoelace tight.

"Well. She could use a break, I think. Maybe she's not the only one?"

Haley straightened up and gave him a blank stare, as if she couldn't imagine what he was talking about.

"Honey. I know Eddie can be a handful, but this is temporary, you know? He's not going to be two forever. You just need to be patient."

"Sure." Gloves in her pockets. Scarf. Sunny came over, her claws clicking on the tile of the kitchen floor. *Why are you putting on your jacket? What's going on? Does it involve me?* She poked her nose under Haley's hands.

"You went to see Jake today? How's he doing?"

"Fine—"

The word barely got out of her mouth before her throat clenched tight. The hot, prickly pressure of tears stung behind her eyes.

An arm in soft, dusty corduroy came around Haley's shoulders, hugging her close. But Haley couldn't relax into the warmth. She couldn't let herself slip. There was that bomb inside her, ticking away.

"Honey." Her father's voice was low and rough. "I know it's hard, but think about everything Jake's gone through. Death's really going to be a mercy for him, when it comes."

"It's *not!*"

Haley yelled it, flinging off her father's arm. Now there was no danger of crying, even though her eyes still stung and her throat hurt so badly it felt like her words were shredding it on their way out.

"So it's *okay?*" she demanded, glaring at her father. "It's just fine that, that—"

"Haley." Now her dad was frowning, and his voice was a warning. "I care about Jake too. You're not the only one who—"

Haley snatched Sunny's leash from the hook by the door and the dog began to fling herself from side to side in the narrow hallway, thumping into Haley's father's knees, nearly knocking him down.

"I better take her out," she muttered, and bent down to grab the scruff of Sunny's neck, clip the leash on her collar as she stood still for a microsecond of quivering impatience, and let the dog drag her out the door.

How could he say that? Haley didn't bother to zip up her coat; her fury was warming enough. She yanked Sunny away from a fascinating stop sign. A mercy? That was just one of those stupid things people said when they didn't want to admit that things were awful. It's God's will. A blessing in disguise. What *crap*.

"Jake's twenty-three," Haley said angrily to Sunny, who looked up intelligently, as if in agreement, and then buried her nose in a drift of leaves. "He's twenty-*three*." Jake hadn't even gotten to finish college. He'd never gone to New York to work in a theater. He'd never traveled to India, to Spain, to all those places he used to talk about. He'd never even seen the last set he'd designed on the stage. And now he wasn't going to do anything but die.

It wasn't a mercy. It wasn't a blessing in disguise. It wasn't anything but horrible. And it wasn't *fair*.

Haley pulled Sunny close by her side and stepped out from the curb. Then she flinched back, grabbing at the dog's leash with both hands. A car swerved; a horn blared. Dirty, gritty air buffeted Haley. Her heel hit the curb and she sat down hard.

Her heart thumped. Dead. She could have been dead. Right there. And Sunny too.

A new grave in the cemetery for her, this time. Neatly marked out with orange nylon rope. Just waiting for someone to come and dig, and then to lower her down.

Haley pulled Sunny close, hugging her tight. The dog leaned into her, panting happily, warm and heavy and solid.

She didn't want to get up. Didn't want to cross the street. Didn't really want to move.

She wanted to stay right here.

It wasn't as if it were so great, sitting alone on a curb on a cold November night, but it was better than what might have happened. Better than just being *gone*.

Rather than that, Haley would sit here forever. Sunny would stay in her arms. Jake would stay alive. Or even better, why not go back a couple of years, before Jake got sick, before Elaine and Eddie arrived in Haley's life. Back to when her mom and dad still laughed together, when Aunt Nell still smiled and drew Haley funny little cards for her birthday and Valentine's Day, back before Haley knew how suddenly and how badly things could change.

Why couldn't everything stay still, as it did once she pressed the shutter of the camera? Frozen, perfect, unchanging.

Why couldn't everything just stay like it was, before?

CHAPTER ELEVEN:
MERCY

My father did not believe it. He would not. But the rumors gathered strength slowly. No other family in our town had been touched by this illness. Only the Browns were sickening and dying, one by one.

There must be a reason.

It's not right. It's not natural.

Each glance of doubt, each worried frown, each whisper—"Have you heard? Do you think? Might it be?"—was, by itself, no more weighty than a snowflake, frail enough to be dissolved by a warm breath. But they gathered, swirling about, until my poor father stood bewildered in the midst of a blizzard, unable to shield himself, unable to hide.

"There are more things in heaven and earth," the minister told him. They sat in the parlor. The rag rug under my father's boots was gray and brown and a faded red. One strand was raveling loose. I'd meant to catch the ragged end, stitch it back in. I'd meant to.

My father sat silent, looking down at the twist of old rag spilling loose onto the painted boards of the floor.

"People are frightened," the minister said. "This is an honest, God-fearing town. They do not understand why God's hand should be so heavy on—on us." He had nearly said "on you."

"God's hand?" My father lifted his head slowly, as if its weight were nearly too much for him. "They dare complain of God's hand? To me? When this plague has taken all my family one by one? Only Patience has survived it. My wife, my daughters, and now—" It's terrible to see a man sob, to see grief overtake rage. His hands were wide in the air, his fingers spread, as if he searched for something to seize and tear limb from limb. "My son!" The words sounded like something croaked by a raven, not shaped by a human tongue.

"My friend." The minister leaned forward. "My old friend. I know. No one has suffered as you have. But that is why I've come to you. *Something* has brought this on us. George." He closed his eyes tightly for the space of a heartbeat. "If prayer cannot deliver us—and, believe me, I have prayed—and if the doctor has no answers, should we not seek elsewhere?"

My father shook his head, but not so much in objection as in bafflement. The snowflakes were around him in a cloud now, stinging and choking, blinding his eyes. "Mercy was a good child. She loved her brother."

"God forbid I should deny it!" His voice was eager, earnest. "But Mercy is gone from us. Her soul is in its true home. But could there be . . ." His voice dropped to a whisper, as if he were ashamed to be overheard. "Could there be . . . something remaining? Some . . . life that is not of the soul, that keeps her heart still beating in the crypt? George, I hate to think it. I hate to imagine such a thing. But Edwin did not sicken before you laid Mercy to rest. You know this is true. If there is a chance, if there is the slightest possibility that anything we can do might stop this—my friend, can we hold back? For Edwin's sake? The boy weakens daily. If he may yet have a chance at life . . ."

My father heaved himself to his feet. He looked as if he would overturn the tables and chairs, rip the pictures and embroidered samplers from the walls, smash vases and windows into fragments.

"I cannot be there," was all he said. "I cannot watch. My daughter—"

"No, no, my friend." The minister seized my father's hands in his. "You must do nothing. We need only your permission. We shall manage it all."

My father did not come to the graveyard. He pulled the curtains shut in Edwin's room.

The ashes of my heart were ground to powder. My sister, Patience, stirred them into sweet wine. No one told Edwin what was in it. By then he was too weak to hold the spoon.

It was not enough to save him.

CHAPTER TWELVE:
HALEY

The house was silent when Haley finally brought Sunny back home. Eddie was, she supposed, asleep. Elaine and her dad must be upstairs. They were probably avoiding her. Since "talking to her" hadn't worked.

Haley snapped the leash off Sunny, and the dog went barreling up the stairs, hoping to find someone new to pet her.

Oh, fine. Traitor of a dog. Couldn't even keep Haley company after Haley had saved her from being dog pancake on the road.

Haley didn't feel like going upstairs to her room. It would just give her dad, or even worse, Elaine, an excuse to "talk" to her again. She flopped down on the couch, hugging her arms tight. Only one lamp was on, across the room, but Haley didn't bother to get up and turn any more lights on.

She'd gotten cold through, sitting for so long on that curb. Now, with her coat off, she could still feel that damp iciness on her skin. It was like having a wet sheet draped over her.

Everything was so quiet. Where were the usual sounds—the refrigerator humming, the furnace grumbling, floorboards creaking underfoot? She couldn't even hear anyone walking around upstairs.

But there was *one* sound. So soft it just teased at the edge of her hearing. Sort of like sitting next to someone who had an iPod turned up too loud. You couldn't hear it properly, but it wouldn't go away, either.

This was just a slow, steady rhythm. Like a drum being hit by a stick wrapped in cotton wool. A light stroke, then a heavier one.

Da-DUM.

Da-DUM.

Haley glanced up to see if someone was walking down the stairs. No one was.

Da-DUM.

Haley looked out the window, but the street outside was empty. No cars or trucks going by.

Old New England houses made a lot of noise, especially as the weather got cold. Haley wriggled herself deeper into the cushions. She could hear the denim of her jeans rub against the soft fabric of the couch.

Da-DUM.

She could hear her breath in her nose. She could hear her own heartbeat.

That's what the quietly nagging noise sounded like. A heartbeat.

No, she wasn't going to think about that.

About Mercy, cold in her crypt, her heart still living, still beating.

No. *No.* That hadn't happened.

Mercy's dead heart, full and glistening with fresh red blood. No way.

Red blood, like those stains on the glove. Like the stains on Haley's hands.

Absolutely not. Haley was just going to stop, stop, *stop* thinking like this—

(*I'll still be dying.*)

Haley put her hands over her ears. But she could still hear the sound, as if the heartbeat was her own now, coming from inside of her—

"Haley? What's wrong?"

Haley jerked her hands away from her ears and stared up at her father, standing beside the couch.

The sound was gone. Just like that. In the basement, the furnace was clunking and groaning into life.

"Okay, stupid question." Her dad sat down heavily near Haley's feet. He stared down at his hands, rough and strong, with clay permanently embedded under the fingernails and in the creases around the knuckles.

"I love Jake too, you know, Haley," he said quietly. "He's my nephew. When his mom died, I—"

Haley could still feel her own heart thumping frantically inside her chest. If she opened her mouth to speak, she was afraid her voice would shake. And then she'd have to tell her dad she'd been scared of—nothing.

But she had to say something. Her dad was looking hard across the room, not blinking. She knew that trick. He was trying not to cry.

"I know," she managed to get out. Her voice sounded hoarse, as if she were getting sick. "I know, Dad."

And he seemed satisfied with that. He nodded. They sat quietly for a moment, until he spoke again.

"Why don't you get upstairs to bed? It's getting late."

Haley wished she could do it: run upstairs with her dad and let him tuck her in, just like when she was little. But that would mean she really was scared. Chased out of her own living room by a spooky noise. No, she couldn't be that dumb.

"Yeah, soon," she said. Her voice sounded more normal this time. "I will."

Her dad patted her feet before heading back up the stairs.

Haley got up and switched on the TV. She needed some noise, something to keep her company. A game show. Perfect. The laughter that spilled out of the set was bright and loud and artificial and not in the least bit spooky. She'd watch this to the end, and then she'd go to bed. That was a perfectly sane, normal, un-frightened thing to do.

She picked her favorite contestant, a woman with slinky black hair who waved frantically at the audience and batted fake black eyelashes at the host. Haley was rooting for her to win a trip to Belize when her eyelids began to get heavy. She blinked, and blinked again, squinting at the colors on the screen through her eyelashes.

Then something cold and wet nudged her arm. A faint whine sounded in her ear. She put out a hand and encountered soft, warm fur.

Scratching Sunny's ears, she tried to orient herself. Why was she so cold? Where was her quilt? She reached down to pull the blankets up to her chin and instead of the soft flannel of her bedspread she felt the slightly scratchy wool of the afghan that usually hung over the back of the couch.

Right, the couch. She'd been watching TV. She must have fallen asleep. Someone had turned the TV off and spread the afghan over her. Someone had switched the lamp off, too. The only light in the room came from the street outside.

Sunny worked her head under Haley's arm, begging for more attention, and Haley sat up, pulling her feet in, leaning back against the arm of the couch.

What time was it? It must be late. The furnace was off, and the house was freezing. Haley half expected to see her breath in the air. She tugged the afghan around her. It made the back of her neck itch. One of Dad's artsy friends had woven it, and it looked great, all deep reds and smoky blues, but it wasn't exactly cozy.

The living room loomed spookily around her, the familiar furniture gone dim and shadowy and somehow bigger. The white light from the window lay across the floor, the bookshelves, the table against the wall, cold and faint as a film of ice. Haley knew she should get up, run upstairs, dive into bed. The thought of flannel sheets and a fleece blanket was luxurious.

But she was reluctant to put her feet on the floor. It felt . . . dangerous. Like it wasn't a good idea to leave her back exposed. Like if she stayed where she was, quiet and unmoving, nothing would notice her. It was the way she'd felt as a kid, huddled under the covers, trying not to stir or breathe. Nothing that lurked in the dark could get you if you stayed perfectly still.

Stupid. She wasn't a little kid anymore. She'd just stand up and walk calmly and quietly up the stairs to her room.

Any minute now.

She would.

Really.

Haley heard a car engine rumble outside. It turned a corner and for a moment glaring light swung through the dark room. Then the car was moving on, red taillights vanishing down the street, leaving Haley blinking and groping for the switch on the lamp beside the couch.

Had she really seen something? She couldn't have. Her cold fingers found the little piece of plastic, twisted it, and warm light filled the room. All the furniture sprang into existence, the shapes and colors and sizes once more familiar, but Haley hardly noticed. She jumped off the couch, the afghan trailing behind her like a cape, and knelt in front of the TV.

Her father liked to watch basketball. The set was a big one, the screen wide and flat and black, filmed over by a layer of dust.

In the dust were faint lines, as if traced by a very light finger. Small curves and loops and circles and vertical strokes. Together they made words.

Patience. Beware.

"Dad? Could you come and—"

"Nathan?" Elaine, with Eddie on one hip and a glass of orange juice in her hand, handed the toddler to her husband. "Take him, would you, honey? I have to find that contract."

"Dad? I wanted to ask you—"

"Hey, monster, come on." Dad got up from the table, bouncing Eddie gently in his arms as the little boy squirmed to get down.

"Dad?"

"Oh, great, oatmeal on the contract." Elaine sorted through papers on the table. "*That* looks professional."

"*Dad!*"

Haley's father and Elaine both turned to look at her.

"What is it?" her dad asked.

"You don't have to shout," Elaine added.

Obviously she *did* have to shout to get anybody's attention, Haley thought, but she didn't say it. "Could you just—come here and look at something? Please."

She led her father, still holding Eddie, into the living room, leaving Elaine bending over the kitchen table, trying to blot oatmeal off her papers with a damp dishcloth.

"So what's up? What am I looking at?" Haley's dad settled Eddie on his hip.

"Just look. Over here."

Haley's gaze fell on the TV screen.

Where, last night, there had been the faint but legible writing, there were now two small handprints in the dust, and streaks and smears across the glass. The letters she'd seen last night had been rubbed out. Haley ran her fingers across the screen, unable to believe it, and stared at the gray smudge on her skin. Eddie had wiped the message away.

"Are you complaining about the quality of the housekeeping?" her father asked. "Because if you are, I'd venture to suggest that you know where the duster is kept."

"No. Uh." Haley knew she sounded like an idiot. "It's just—I thought there was something wrong with the TV. Last night."

Her father reached down to turn the TV on. A commercial for zit cream blared out into the room. He flipped through a few channels.

"Works okay now, anyway." Her father gave Haley an inquiring look. "Is that what you wanted to show me?"

Haley felt her face growing hot. "Uh, yeah, I—okay, fine," she mumbled.

Maybe it had never been real. Could she have dreamed that she'd woken up and seen the headlights slicing through the room, seen the warning in the dust? The memory was sharp and clear, not fuzzy at the edges, like a dream remembered in the morning. But once she'd dreamed that she'd gotten out of bed to finish some uncompleted homework, and it had seemed so real that she'd been sitting in math class looking down at a blank worksheet before she'd realized that she hadn't actually done the problems.

It was stupid, anyway. She shouldn't have tried to tell her dad anything. Because if she wasn't going crazy, if she hadn't been dreaming, and if somebody was trying to send her some kind of message, then there obviously wasn't much she was supposed to do about it. *Patience. Beware.* All that seemed to be saying was that she should keep alert and wait.

Her dad was still looking at her funny. Thankfully, Elaine provided a distraction. "Haley?" she called from the kitchen. "Do you have that stuff ready?"

"What stuff?"

Elaine appeared in the door, her briefcase in one hand. "I asked you twice already this morning," she said, amused and irritated. "Here, Nathan, I'll take him." She held out her arms for Eddie. "If you've got that stuff ready to take back to your aunt's, I can drop it off before I take Eddie to playgroup. But I'm leaving as soon as I've got his coat on."

That stuff for Aunt Brown? The newspaper clippings, the family tree, Mercy's glove.

"Oh. Oh yeah!" Haley backed toward the hallway. "Thanks, Elaine, I'll get it right now; thanks, really!" She bolted up the stairs.

The glove, Haley thought. The first spooky thing that had happened had been those bloody stains on the glove. Then the sound like the heartbeat, the writing in the dust—it had all happened since she'd brought Mercy's glove into the house.

So she'd just get that glove *out* of the house. And even if there was nothing to be afraid of—which Haley was sure there wasn't, because it would be crazy to think like that, and she didn't exactly need to go crazy now, not with everything else that was going on—even if there was *nothing* creepy about having a dead vampire's glove in her room, she'd feel a lot better once it was somewhere else.

Haley was prepared to look all over her room for the red box with the glove inside, prepared to have it trying to hide itself under her pillows or in her dresser drawers, but there it was, sitting meekly on her desk, on top of the envelope with Aunt Brown's papers. She snatched both up.

Underneath was the family tree, the one she'd messed up and had to redraw.

Hadn't she thrown this away? She thought she had. But it was smooth and un-crumpled now, sitting on her desk.

There was Mercy's name. Mercy and her sister, Grace, also dead, and little Edwin. And one other name. Mercy's sister, the only child who'd survived.

Patience Brown.

Underneath Mercy's name were the dates of her birth and death. Edwin's and Grace's also. Patience had a birth date too. 1868. She'd been five years older than Mercy.

But no date of death.

Patience wasn't only a virtue, Haley thought, staring down at the family tree. It was also a name.

CHAPTER THIRTEEN:
HALEY

All day long, the feel of the piece of paper in her pocket nagged at Haley. She'd folded the family tree up small, and the sharp corners poked her leg every time she moved.

In each class she eyed the trash can by the door. But somehow she could never quite make up her mind to throw the thing away.

In History, the reports on ancestors were over. Mr. Samuelson was droning on about the War of 1812. Haley slipped the paper out of her pocket and flattened it on her desk.

What did it tell her? Nothing.

She ran her finger along Patience's name. No date of death. What did that mean?

Probably nothing. A mistake. Aunt Brown forgot to write it down.

Aunt Brown forgot? Haley was pretty sure Aunt Brown never forgot anything.

Well, then, Haley had made the mistake. That was much more likely. It wasn't like it *meant* something.

It wasn't like Patience had never . . . died.

Somebody kicked her foot. Hard. Haley jerked her head up.

Mr. Samuelson was standing at the whiteboard, a marker in his hand.

"Francis Scott Key," whispered a voice from behind her.

"Francis Scott Key?" Haley repeated hopefully.

"Correct." Mr. Samuelson gave her a slightly suspicious look and wrote the name on the board. "And yes, thank you, Kevin, *what* exactly was Mr. Key so famous for?"

Haley glanced back over her shoulder. Alan O'Neil met her eyes and grinned.

Haley crumpled the family tree up. When the bell rang, she got to the door as quickly as she could. A blue recycling bin was by her knee. She would just throw the family tree in there and forget about it. Right now.

"So what was so interesting?" Alan's voice was at her shoulder. "Can I see?"

"No!" Haley squeezed the piece of paper into a tighter ball, crushing it in her hand. "I mean—nothing. It's—um. Thanks. For back there."

"You okay?"

"Fine." Haley didn't dare throw the family tree away now. Alan might see it, or anyone might pick it up, and then—

"Sorry, I have to go somewhere. Else." Embarrassment was about to crush her. She'd collapse in on herself, a little black hole of humiliation.

"But you've got lunch, don't you?" Alan looked bewildered.

"Haley? You okay?" Mel was at her other side.

"Fine!" Haley yelped. It had been bad enough looking like an idiot in front of her dad this morning, but now, in front of Alan O'Neil?

"Have to take some pictures," she gabbled. "For the paper. You know? Just outside, just around, the lunchroom, that kind of—"

Nobody in all those horror movies ever mentioned *embarrassment* as a peril of being haunted, she thought, as more meaningless words spurted out of her mouth. Monsters who rip you limb from limb, vampires who suck your blood, demons who steal your soul, sure. But nobody tells you about the possibly fatal danger of looking like an idiot.

She fled. She stayed carefully out of sight, even though it meant eating her sandwich perched on a windowsill in the girls' bathroom.

This was ridiculous. She had to *do* something. Something to get all of this out of her head.

Swallowing the last bite of her turkey sandwich, licking mustard off her upper lip, Haley made up her mind. After school was over, she killed time in the office for the school newspaper, fiddling around with the layout as if she actually had some new photos to put in. She finally met up with Mel again once Mel's Amnesty International meeting was over. They stood on the steps in front of the school, Mel pulling on her gloves and Haley zipping up her jacket. And, in her head, Haley heard the conversation they were about to have.

Mel, would you come back to the cemetery with me?

Why?

To see if somebody named Patience is really dead.

It wasn't going to go well. But Haley couldn't help herself. The words were lifting off her tongue and nudging against her teeth. No matter how stupid it was going to sound, she wanted some company. She wanted her best friend.

"Mel, listen . . . "

"Hey. You going anywhere?"

Alan O'Neil, a pair of soccer cleats hanging over his shoulder, had turned back from a group of his friends. He'd definitely turned back, Haley thought, analyzing the moment. Spun around quickly, as if he wasn't giving himself too much time to think, and taken a couple of steps so he could talk to them. It wasn't like he'd just said hi in passing. He'd made an effort.

"Hey, no, we're not doing anything, really."

"Actually, we—"

Mel and Haley spoke together. Mel looked over at Haley in surprise.

"We're going over to Starbucks," Alan said, jerking his head at the friends waiting for him on the sidewalk. "You want to come?"

Was he asking one of them out and the other one just to come along? But he was talking to both of them, looking at both of them. If the invitation was meant more for one than the other, it was impossible to say which.

Mel was addicted to Frappuccinos. She grinned widely. "Yeah, really? Sure, let's go."

"I can't."

They both looked at Haley.

"I mean, there's something I have to—"

Haley stopped. Maybe she could have said something to Mel. No way she was going to look stupid twice in one day in front of Alan.

"What do you have to do?" Mel had walked down a couple of steps, but she turned to look up at Haley.

"Just—something." Haley shifted her backpack on her shoulder. "You guys go on, though. Go without me."

"Are you going over to Jake's? Again?"

"No." Too late, Haley realized that she ought to have said *yes*. That would have been the perfect excuse.

But it would also have been a lie. Another lie. To Mel, who'd been her best friend since second grade.

"What is it, then? Come on. You never—wait a minute, okay?" Mel said to Alan. Then she ran back to Haley, grabbed her arm, and pulled her up a couple more steps.

The conversation that came next happened in hot, angry whispers.

"You never do *anything* anymore, Haley!"

"I do so. I was going to the mall!"

"But you didn't."

"That wasn't my fault!"

"And yesterday you just disappeared. I waited for you after school. You never said—"

"So now I have to check in?"

"I know stuff's going on, but—"

"Stuff!" Was that the way Mel thought of it? Just *stuff*? It wasn't like Haley could tell her all of it—the glove, the heartbeat, the writing in the dust, the family tree in her pocket—but didn't Mel get it? What Haley was dealing with? "It's not just *stuff*!"

"I know. I know that, but you can't just—" Mel flapped her gloved hand.

"And I've got something to *do*. It's more important than some stupid Frappuccino! You don't understand!"

"Yes, I do!"

Haley was shocked into silence by the anger in Mel's voice. Mel never got mad. Mel cared about her dead grandmother and about sparrows and about people in jail in faraway countries with unpronounceable names. And now Mel was really mad? Mel was really mad at *her*?

"I do understand, Haley." Her words were sharp and bright and shiny as knives. "You know I do. Or you would if you spent five minutes thinking about somebody besides yourself!"

And Mel walked down the steps toward Alan and his friends, leaving Haley alone.

So now Haley was going to visit a graveyard for a second time, this time alone, with the sun dipping closer to the horizon than before. Wonderful. In horror movies, this was the kind of thing that got people killed.

But this wasn't a horror movie, Haley told herself. It was her life. Okay, things had gotten a little strange lately. That didn't mean there was any real *danger* in the old cemetery. That monsters were going to leap out from behind a tree and devour her.

No. It didn't. Definitely not. Even if she was all on her own as she leaned her bike against the fence and walked through the wrought-iron gate.

Well, not completely on her own. She did have an eager-to-please golden retriever for protection. After Mel had walked off with Alan, Haley had gone home to get Sunny. At least Sunny, now panting happily after running down the streets alongside Haley's bike, wouldn't dump her for a guy.

She couldn't believe Mel had acted like that. As if she didn't know. As if she didn't care.

A flock of tiny brown sparrows burst up from the grass and zipped past Haley's head. Their little wings moved so quickly they blurred as the birds swooped and dipped toward a nearby tree.

Someone had scattered fresh birdseed on one of the graves. Haley could guess who.

(I do understand, Haley.)

Even so. Even so, Mel didn't have to go off and leave her.

Except that Haley had told her to.

Fine. Haley realized that she'd stopped, staring after the little birds. She pulled Sunny's leash and starting walking again.

Maybe Mel *did* have a point. Maybe it wasn't fair to be so angry at her.

But nothing was fair anymore, was it? So why couldn't Haley get a little mad now and them? At Mel. At her mom, for not doing Thanksgiving properly. At her dad, or Elaine, because all they cared about was Eddie. And that definitely wasn't fair, Haley knew it wasn't fair, and she really, really didn't care.

Because it wasn't like she could be mad at . . .

It wasn't Jake's *fault*, after all. He didn't choose to get sick.

(*He chose to pick up that cigarette, though, didn't he? He chose to come home from the hospital.*)

Now the light was starting to fade from the cloudy sky in a pale, washed-out sunset of bleached pink and faint peach. Haley's camera was in her pocket. She slipped it out and took a shot of a sad-faced stone angel, with that ethereal light behind her.

The last sliver of the sun melted away behind the trees like butter on a hot skillet. But the sky was still bright, and there was plenty of light to see by. Sunny trotted calmly at Haley's side as she put the camera away and walked on.

(*He's only twenty-three. He could have stayed in the hospital. He could have tried . . .*)

The old willow leaned over the Brown family headstones, its branches bare and empty against the deepening blue of the sky.

(*He said he tried for a long time.*

Not long enough.)

None of the stones were for Patience. Haley worked her way out from Mercy's grave. Edwin, Grace, Mary, George.

(*He acts like it doesn't matter. He makes these stupid jokes, like it's all just—nothing. A punch line. Like being gone forever doesn't scare him.*)

She looked further, out into distant cousins and aunts and uncles. More Marys. Elizabeth. Anne. Jane and Janet, sisters. Theodore and Allister, brothers. Name after name, cut into old, pale-gray stone. But no Patience.

What did that prove? Nothing. For all Haley knew there was a grave somewhere else. Maybe Patience got married. Maybe she was buried with her husband's family. Maybe she moved to Alaska to pan for gold or to China as a missionary and was buried there, a neat headstone somewhere far away.

And even if Haley *had* found a grave, what would that have meant? What would she have done then?

(I need him. Doesn't he get that? Dad and Elaine are too busy with Eddie. Mom's off in New York, and maybe she'll really notice me when I'm good enough to have something to hang on the walls of her gallery. And even Mel . . .)

Mel had been Haley's best friend forever. But that didn't mean she was family.

Not like Jake.

CHAPTER FOURTEEN:
MERCY

S he doesn't know.

    I tried to warn her. But I can't do much. She's the one who will have to do something.

I have to find a way. I have to make her see.

CHAPTER FIFTEEN

HALEY

Haley rested one hand on a tombstone, the cool stone smooth under her fingers.

Family. The same blood in your veins, the same DNA coiled in every cell of your body. Haley remembered the family tree, the branches stretching back through the years. Browns connected to each other, in life and even in . . .

Well. In death. That was what a place like this meant, wasn't it? That family was family, dead or alive.

"Um . . ." She cleared her throat and glanced around to be sure nobody could hear her. The graveyard was deserted.

Sunny sat down on her haunches, wagged her tail once, and looked expectantly at Haley. *What now?* her eyes said.

"Um. Mercy?"

It was stupid. But there was nobody to see her being stupid, so that was okay.

Family was family, a tangled web of connection, blood and nerves and genes and emotion stretching back over years and years. And Mercy was part of Haley's family, just like Jake, so

maybe all the strange things that kept happening meant that
Mercy had something to say.

Then, okay. Haley would listen.

"Mercy? I'm here. If you want to . . ."

Nothing. A cold breeze stirred the twigs of the leafless
birches and ruffled the long grass at their roots. Haley's fingers
and ears and the tip of her nose grew colder. Sunny scratched at
her ear, jangling her collar, and the sweet, chilly, metallic sound
drifted across the graveyard.

Stupid. This whole thing was stupid.

"Come on, Sunny." Haley tugged at the leash. Disappointment curdled in her stomach. Disappointment? Why? Shouldn't
she be *happy* that she wasn't getting visited from beyond the
grave? That her life was just her life, not some idiotic horror
movie?

It didn't make any sense for her to feel let down. Just like it
didn't make any sense to be mad at her own cousin for something he couldn't help.

She couldn't be mad at Jake. She really couldn't. Because
that would make her a horrible person. She couldn't—hate him.
For making dumb jokes and smoking—smoking—how disgusting. And for going away and leaving her.

Haley slid the hand that wasn't holding Sunny's leash into
her jacket pocket and felt her camera there. She took it out. The
light was going, but she'd take one last shot of Mercy's grave.
Sort of a good-bye.

She turned on the camera and centered Mercy's headstone
in the viewscreen. She tipped the camera a little, and then
dropped it. It hit the soft damp grass without a sound.

Haley fell to her hands and knees, scrabbling after the
camera.

She'd imagined it. Hadn't she? Some trick of the fading light had created what she thought she'd seen—dark eyes wide in a pale face, a mouth that might sob or shriek.

Haley's trembling fingers closed around the little metal box. She sat back on her heels and raised the camera hesitantly, aiming it at Mercy's grave once more, and then looked into the viewscreen again.

The face was there, framed by dark hair. Haley's gaze went quickly to the actual grave, but there was nothing to be seen. Nothing except the stone that had stood there quietly for more than a century.

But on the viewscreen, the face rushed toward her, the mouth opening, the eyes full of desperation. Haley fell back, flat on the damp grass, her arms flying up to fight off the thing that was leaping on her.

Except that nothing did. Nothing touched her. She sat up and got shakily to her hands and knees, stuffing her camera quickly into her pocket.

And then she felt it. The faint vibrations rose up through the ground. She felt them in her legs, in her outstretched hands.

Da-DUM.

Da-DUM.

This time the sound didn't just tease at the edge of her hearing. This time it was loud, heavy, rhythmic pounding, and it sounded to Haley as if it would never stop.

Sunny sat down beside her, wagged her tail, and panted happily into Haley's face.

Stupid dog. Haley shoved herself to her feet, grabbed the leash, and ran.

At the gate she stopped, pulling Sunny close. The sound had faded, left behind at Mercy's grave.

Gritting her teeth, Haley turned. But there was nothing behind her. Nothing had chased her; nothing was reaching out to grab her. Nothing but her own fear, which clutched her in long, icy fingers.

What was *happening* to her? Was she being haunted? Was she being—she took a few shaky steps to put her back against the cemetery fence—*hunted*?

They'd said that Mercy would not stay dead. They'd said that her heart, beating within her corpse, had sucked the life from her own family.

Haley had thought it was nothing but a quaint old New England tradition. She had called it ignorance and superstition and fear. But Mercy's family and friends and neighbors—could they actually have been right?

And was somebody walking down the driveway of Aunt Brown's house?

Haley blinked and looked again. The light was fading fast now and there were no streetlights on this road, so she couldn't see details. But the long skirt, the straight back, the quick steps that seemed to cover more ground than they should—she knew them.

Aunt Brown? That was impossible.

Sunny pulled back hard on the leash, yanking Haley off balance. Retreating, the dog tugged Haley into the shadow of a large monument. Under the shadow of a stone angel's wings, Sunny crowded against Haley, almost sitting on her feet, and whimpered. Without thinking, Haley knelt to pull the dog close and clamp one hand around her muzzle. Somehow she felt it would be a bad idea to make any noise right now.

"Shhh," she whispered. "Shhh, it's okay . . . "

Hugging Sunny, she peered back around the monument.

The figure in the long skirt was now walking briskly down the road. Haley could see more clearly now—the long hair brushed smoothly back to a knot on the back of the head, the cardigan over the white blouse. It was Aunt Brown, and she walked as if she knew exactly where she was going and was in a hurry to get there.

Haley gritted her teeth. Beside her, Sunny whined. There was no sense huddling here in a graveyard. It was just Aunt Brown, after all, and if she were out for a walk, that was weird, maybe, but not exactly scary.

So stop being scared, Haley ordered herself. *Stand up.*

After a little while, she did. She peered around the stone angel. Nothing.

Nothing? How could there be nothing?

There was no sign of the quickly moving figure in the long skirt. The road ran long and straight past the cemetery, and there was not a single person on it. But nobody could have moved that fast. Certainly not an old lady who hadn't left her house in Haley's lifetime.

Who everybody *thought* hadn't left the house.

Haley stood up cautiously, holding Sunny's leash.

What should she do? She had no idea. Go rushing home to her dad and Elaine, telling them . . . what? That a dead woman had written messages on a television screen? That she'd seen a face on her camera's screen and heard a heart beating in a grave? They'd have her talking to a psychiatrist so fast her head would-n't have *time* to spin.

Should she call Mel? But it would be the same problem. The same pity. The same sweet and sympathetic disbelief.

There was only one person who'd always listened to her. Haley tied Sunny's leash to the handlebars of her bike and set off down the street as fast as the dog could run.

Her dad and Elaine would be expecting her back for dinner, but she could call them from Jake's.

Haley was panting as hard as Sunny by the time she reached Jake's street, and the last of the light had faded from the sky. The cold, dry air hurt her lungs and made her cough.

She had her own key to the front door of Jake's apartment building. Sunny flopped down on the cold concrete of the front walk to rest as Haley shook the key free from the others on her ring and slipped it into the lock.

But as she turned the key, Sunny suddenly jumped up and yelped, yanking Haley's arm. The keys dropped to the doormat with a muffled clank.

"Sunny! What—? Ow, quit it!" Haley bent down to pick up the keys and the dog nearly pulled her over. She was barking now, loudly. "*Stop* it!" Haley insisted, giving the leash a good pull to bring Sunny back to her side. "Hold still—come on, quit making this so hard." She grabbed Sunny's collar with her left hand, using all her strength to keep the dog from moving, and turned the key in the lock with her right.

Sunny resisted as Haley dragged her into the lobby, and redoubled her barking. Oh, great. Neighbors were going to be looking out of the doors any minute now to see what was up. Jake might even appear, laughing as Haley wrestled the dog down the hallway, claws scrabbling and slipping on the linoleum.

At least Jake's apartment was on the ground floor. She wouldn't have to drag Sunny up the stairs.

In front of Jake's door, she clung to Sunny with one hand and shook out her key ring with the other, trying to find the right key. But then Sunny growled, and the sound was so fierce that Haley dropped her collar and actually flinched away. She'd never heard Sunny make a sound like that.

Sunny's upper lip was pulling away from her teeth, the fur on the back of her neck was bristling, and suddenly she seemed to change her mind about not wanting to go near Jake's apartment. With a single-minded ferocity, she lunged for the door.

Haley, expecting to see her bounce off the wood, was caught off guard when the door crashed open. The leash, still looped around her wrist, went taut, and Haley was dragged inside.

The room was dark, not a light on anywhere. A rug slid under Sunny's feet and nearly tripped Haley. The leash went slack for a moment and slipped over Haley's hand. Sunny's barking was a torrent of sound, battering the walls of the little room, battering the thoughts out of Haley's head.

She couldn't think, but she could still see.

The only light in the room came from the window, spilling in from the streetlight outside. Jake's armchair was by that window. Haley could see his shape outlined in it, as if he'd fallen asleep there, his legs stretched out, his head leaning back.

Something straightened up, something that had been bending over him. For half a second Haley saw it, outlined against the dimly lit rectangle of the window. A thin, upright figure. Hair smooth against the skull, a long dress. Her mind took the picture like her camera took a photo. *Click.*

And the figure vanished from the window, gone like a shred of mist snatched by the wind. Something slammed into Haley, something as heavy and solid as iron. She didn't feel herself falling; she only felt herself hitting the floor. It almost felt like the floor hitting her, a thump that knocked the breath out of her.

A gust of clammy air blew in her face, a smell choked her— clay, earth, something foul, rotten, buried deep. A vision sparked in Haley's mind, lit up as if with a flash on a dark night—white maggots, pallid and damp, crawling blindly over something black and crumbling, writhing, squirming, eating hungrily—

Icy fingers grabbed hold of Haley's face. Something stung her cheek, a thin, distant pain. Haley forced a breath into her lungs and shrieked Jake's name just as a siren screamed outside and a red blade of light stabbed into the room.

One of the neighbors, it turned out, had heard Sunny's frantic barking, had seen the door to Jake's apartment swinging open, and had called the police. That much Haley understood later, when the room was full of light and noise and people. Police officers in uniforms, a couple of neighbors, two EMTs who put a bandage on a bloody cut on Jake's neck, just under the corner of the jaw.

Maybe a knife, one of the policemen had said, coming over to look and take a photograph of the wound before the bandage was taped down. Although the knife must have been pretty blunt, she added, to make a cut as ragged as that.

"You should see your doctor for a tetanus shot," the EMT said as she smoothed the gauze into place. "If you're sure you don't want to come to the ER now?"

"I'm sure." Jake's face looked sickly pale, but his voice was steady.

"Miss?" A policeman holding a notebook turned his attention to Haley. Haley had been told his name and had promptly forgotten it. "You can't add anything to your description? Hair color? Eyes?"

"The light was off. It was dark." Haley hugged her arms across her chest. Her voice was less steady than Jake's.

"Height? She was standing against the window, you said. How high did she come up?"

Haley measured a spot on the window frame with her hand. "About to here, I think."

The police officer quirked a slightly skeptical eyebrow. "But strong, you said?"

That force slamming into her, that hand on her face, those fingers like cold iron—Haley touched the sore spots on her jaw gently. "Yes. Strong."

She knew why the officer had lifted his eyebrow. The spot she'd touched on the window frame would make Jake's attacker only a few inches over five feet. She'd already described her as a woman, thin, slightly built. How could somebody like that have hit her with such force?

"Well, addicts looking for a fix—they can surprise you." The officer shrugged. Haley stared at a mole, a dark blotch near the corner of his eye, as if it had hypnotized her. "We'll talk to the neighbors, see if anybody saw her on the streets. And we'll be back in a few days to see you both again. Meanwhile, don't fall asleep again without locking the door. Medications can bring a good price on the streets."

"I thought I—well. Obviously I didn't. Lock it. I will." Jake rubbed a hand over his face. The EMT who'd put the bandage on glanced at him, frowning a little. Then she looked at Haley.

"What's that on your face?"

Haley blinked and put her hand up to her cheek. She stared in surprise at the blood on her fingertips and looked down to see a few small spots of red sprinkled over the front of her white T-shirt.

There was the sharp sting of alcohol as the EMT cleaned the scratch, then smeared it with a sticky ointment and stuck a bandage over it. The room emptied out, neighbors telling Jake to call if he needed anything, the EMT reminding him of a tetanus shot. When they had all gone, Haley shut the door behind them, locked it, and turned the dead bolt. Its heavy, satisfying metallic clunk was the sound of safety.

Except that Jake thought he'd locked the door before . . .

Jake was leaning back in his chair, eyes half closed. The white bandage didn't stand out as it should have against his skin.

"You okay?" he asked.

Haley nodded. She couldn't be sure he'd seen her, so she put it into words. "I'm fine."

"Liar."

"Yeah." Haley's nerves were twitching and jumping, her body fizzing with adrenaline and shock. That hand on her face. That stench. And later, when she'd slapped the lights on, Jake sitting up, staring blankly at her as if he didn't know who she was, with blood running down his neck.

"I'm staying," Haley said firmly. She called home, told her father and Elaine what had happened, told them she and Jake were both fine. The big Band-Aid the EMT had stuck over her face tugged at her skin and her jaw ached with talking before she'd explained it all, and they'd agreed that since it was a Friday and there was no school the next day, she could stay overnight.

When she hung up the phone, Jake was asleep in his chair.

Haley pulled him up by one arm and steered him over to the bed. She knelt to pull his shoes off and heard a long, drawn-out whine from under the bed.

"Sunny?" Haley bent down to look and Sunny poked her head out, a wisp of dust clinging to her nose. She huddled against the floor, as if hoping to melt into the wood. Even her fur seemed limp, and her ears dropped against her head.

"What a guard dog." Jake's voice was faint. "Defending her master against all danger . . . "

By the time Haley had coaxed Sunny out into the room, Jake was nearly asleep again. The dog nosed frantically at his hand, lying limp on top of the sheets, and he stirred enough to rub her ears.

"S'okay, mutt, you're not a Doberman or anything."

"Jake?" Haley, still sitting on the floor, looked up.

"Mmmm?"

"Are you sure you don't want to go to the hospital? You look . . . "

"I've really spent enough time in hospitals, Haley."

"Listen, there's something—" Haley faltered. But Jake waited patiently, not moving or speaking, for her to go on. "I think maybe something weird is going on. I don't know. Can I tell you? Do you promise not to laugh or—"

Jake's quiet, deep breathing was her only answer. Haley sighed. She covered him with a blanket and took the one folded at the foot of his bed for herself. Curled up in Jake's armchair, her feet tucked under her, the blanket wrapped around her shoulders, she found that her eyes wouldn't close. She didn't know how long she stayed awake, staring into the dark.

CHAPTER SIXTEEN:
HALEY

In the morning, in Jake's bathroom, Haley splashed water on her face and peeled the bandage from her cheek. The scratch from last night had healed really quickly. She rubbed her fingers over the smooth, wet skin. No soreness. No scar.

She was glad now that she hadn't told Jake about her suspicions last night. In the light of day it all seemed ridiculous. What had happened out at the cemetery was bizarre, sure, but maybe nothing more than her nerves and imagination. After all, what proof did she have? A message on a dusty TV screen that might have been a dream? A spooky sound in a cemetery?

And somebody breaking into Jake's apartment—but that had nothing to do with any of it. Probably just an addict after Jake's medications, like the policeman said.

Certainly not what she'd been halfway to thinking last night, seeing Jake with blood on his throat, thinking back to that dark figure bent over him, outlined in the dim gray light from the window. Thinking of Mercy, so hungry for life that, even in her grave, she'd taken it. Stolen it from the people who'd loved her most.

Of course not. She'd have to be crazy to think that in Exeter, Rhode Island, in the twenty-first century, there could be such a thing as—

Her brain got as far as the "v" and then quit, out of pure shame. Haley saw her face in the mirror turn red.

"Vampires." She forced herself to whisper the word out loud, as a punishment for stupidity, and watched her blush grow deeper.

Vampires. Great, Haley, just great. What would be next— monsters under the bed?

She dropped her eyes from the image in the mirror and squeezed some toothpaste onto her finger, rubbed her teeth, and hurried out of the bathroom.

Jake looked better that morning, a little color back in his face. "So I never asked you." He leaned against the kitchen counter. The hand that held a mug of his pomegranate tea to his lips barely trembled. "Why you came by last night?"

"Just. Uh. Bringing Sunny for a visit." Haley made a big fuss of finding her jacket, shaking it out, putting it on.

"Glad you did, anyway." If Jake suspected she wasn't being quite truthful, he didn't seem inclined to push her. "Haley. Wait a minute."

Near the door, Haley looked back.

"You probably saved my life," he said. "What's left of it, anyway."

Haley felt a shivery jolt deep in her stomach. Why did he have to put it like that? What was she supposed to say?

"Sorry. I know you don't like jokes."

Haley looked at her cousin, leaning against the counter, smiling a little, absentmindedly rubbing at the bandage on his neck, as if it itched. But she was seeing him slumped in his chair last night, blood on his neck, soaking into his shirt. She'd thought that was it. She'd thought he was gone.

And the last time she'd seen him, she'd—

"I'm sorry I yelled," she said hoarsely. "About you smoking. About—"

"Didn't I tell you?" Jake interrupted her. "It's fine if you're not fine. It's okay if you get mad. If you yell."

But not at you, Haley thought.

"Even at me. I'm not going to come back and haunt you, just because you got pissed off one time. Or two. Or twenty."

Haley flinched. But Jake was taking a big swallow of his tea and didn't notice.

"You can hate me when I'm gone," he added, putting the mug down on the counter. His smile, like the rest of him, looked thin and tired. Worn out. Like there just wasn't much of him left. "If you have to. It's okay. I promise. It's fine."

Haley opened the kitchen door and stared blankly at her dad, Elaine, and Mel, who all sat at the table, looking just as blankly back at her. She felt as if she'd accidentally walked into the wrong house. And the lost, bewildered feeling didn't go away, even as they all jumped up and crowded around her, hugging her, patting Sunny, asking questions, telling her how Mel had called last night, and Elaine had told her what had happened, and Mel had been worried and had come over early this morning to be sure Haley was okay.

Haley sat down, took a mug of hot chocolate that Elaine handed her, and answered questions as best she could, considering how little she knew—how little anybody knew. Break-in. After drugs, maybe. Knife.

"And the police? What did the police say?" Her dad sounded almost angry, which was rare. Haley looked at his scowl in confusion.

"To lock the door. They're coming back later."

"To lock the door? Great. That's great advice."

"But Jake's okay?" Elaine interjected, putting a gentle hand on her husband's arm. Haley nodded. "Thank God you both are," Elaine said, reaching out to hug Haley. "Are you sure, honey?" She pulled back a little to look at Haley's face and brushed cool fingers against her stepdaughter's cheek. "You look . . ."

Like I've seen a ghost. Haley finished the sentence inside her head.

Had she? Had she seen a ghost?

Because that wasn't *so* crazy, was it? That wasn't as insane as thinking vampires were wandering around Rhode Island.

Jake could make jokes about coming back to haunt her, but what if it wasn't a joke? Jake had said she could hate him when he was gone. But what if it were the other way around? What if Mercy was the one who was still here, hating the people who had called her a monster and cut out her heart? What if she had been waiting a hundred years for revenge on her own family?

"Like you barely slept." Elaine finished her sentence and gestured at her husband. "Come on, Nathan. You're going to help me clean up that closet upstairs."

"I am? Now? But—"

"Haley, there are some of those cinnamon rolls you like in the fridge. Get one for Mel. Nathan, let's go. Eddie won't stay asleep for much longer and I want to get that cupboard straightened out."

"You said closet."

"Whatever." Elaine nearly pushed Haley's dad out of the kitchen.

"What's up with them?" Haley stared after her father and stepmother.

"Um." Mel's cheeks were pink. "I think she thinks we want to talk."

"We do?"

"I kind of told her we had a fight."

"We did?"

Of course they'd had a fight. Haley just hadn't thought about it, exactly. Not after what had happened at the cemetery, and then at Jake's.

(*You can hate me when I'm gone.*)

"I'm so, so sorry, Haley," Mel was babbling. "Don't be mad, okay? Because I—"

At the cemetery, Haley remembered, before her search for Patience's grave, before that face in her camera, before the heartbeat echoing up out of the ground, there had been something else, something that had made her think of Mel—a little flock of brown sparrows, their wings blurring in the air.

"I'm not mad," she said to Mel. "It's fine."

"Because I didn't mean to. It just kind of—" Mel's cheeks were getting pinker and pinker.

"You were right. I'm not the only person—"

"And he did like you, he really did, only—"

"I didn't mean to act like that. I know you miss her."

"—he thought you weren't interested, and then we were sort of talking, and we kept on talking, and—"

"Who thought? You were talking?"

"Miss who?"

The two separate conversations they had been having collided, and it took a lot of words to sort through the wreckage.

Somehow Haley found herself reassuring Mel that she didn't like Alan O'Neil, well, she liked him, but she only liked him, and it was fine if Mel wanted to go out with him. No, she didn't mind, it was fine.

"But do you think—" she started to ask.

"Oh, good." Mel was smiling now, pinker than ever. "And we'll all hang out, you know? We won't get all gross and couple-y or anything. And—"

"—that someone might come back?"

"Come back? From where?" Mel looked completely bewildered.

"You know. Like your grandmother. Someone—gone." Haley kept her eyes on the table. She didn't want to see Mel's face.

"Like *Gran?*"

But Haley could hear the disbelief in her best friend's voice. And then she could hear the pity.

"Haley, you mean—like Jake?"

"No! Not like Jake, like—well, like Mercy."

"Haley, really, are you still thinking about that? Because it's kind of—"

"No, just listen. Okay? Listen." Haley knew she shouldn't have asked. Now she was stuck, she'd have to explain, but every word was just making things worse. "If they're—not like some stupid horror movie or something, but if they're angry, if things weren't—right—could they, kind of, somehow, *stay?* For revenge, or something? Do you think?"

There was an awful pause.

"No," Mel said.

Haley stared down at her mug of hot chocolate.

"People just—I don't know what happens, Haley, I really don't, if there's Heaven or something or just nothing, but I know they don't *stay*. I know Gran—not for *that*."

The hot chocolate had gone cold. There was a scum of cocoa on top of the milk.

116

"I read about this stuff all the time, for Amnesty—people being tortured, horrible things, Haley, you can't imagine, and just locked up for years and years. And sometimes they die. But they don't hang around figuring out ways to hurt the people who hurt them. I know they don't, Haley. Only the living do that."

Haley shut the door to her room behind her. A glance out of the window revealed Mel making her way down the front path, and stopping to throw her last bite of cinnamon roll to a crow on the lawn.

She'd finally told Mel she was tired. That was true, anyway. She hadn't slept much in Jake's armchair.

Did one small truth balance out one big lie? Probably not.

But she couldn't have told Mel the truth. She couldn't have said *no*. That it wasn't fine at all. That the thought of Alan and Mel talking all afternoon—Alan asking Mel out—Alan kissing Mel—made her feel strange. Disconnected and shaky. As if the last line connecting her to Earth had snapped, and now she was drifting free. With no idea of how she'd ever get down again.

Just one more person. One more person who'd walked away from her.

And the worst part was, she'd actually told him to. "*You guys go on. Go without me.*" She'd said it. And they'd done it.

Haley had to add *stupid* to the list of things she was feeling.

Her mouth tasted of sour milk; her clothes she had slept in felt stale on her skin. Maybe she'd feel better if she changed and brushed her teeth for real.

Her purple fleece shirt was clean, but there were no jeans in her drawer. Elaine would say that was because she hadn't gotten her clothes as far as the laundry basket. Haley snagged a pair of pants from the floor. Jeans that had been worn for a few days were softer and more comfortable anyway.

She slid her hands into the pockets to make the jeans hang right off her hips and felt something there, something smooth and cool. She fished it out.

It was the silver chain she'd found on the floor of Jake's apartment. Maia had distracted her, and she'd forgotten about slipping it into her pocket.

Haley trailed the chain through her fingers. It was strange, now that she came to think about it. If it wasn't Maia's—if it wasn't Elaine's—whose was it, then?

Jake didn't have a lot of visitors, after all. And this necklace must belong to someone he knew. Someone who hadn't noticed when the clasp broke and the chain fell to the floor. Someone who'd been standing right next to his chair, maybe even leaning over him—

And in Haley's mind, something went *click*. A silver chain against a white blouse. She'd seen it before.

Haley snatched up her camera from her desk, clicked back through the images. It hadn't been a good photo. She hadn't transferred it over to the laptop. Had she deleted it?

No. She hadn't.

Aunt Brown's face was blurred. She'd moved just as Haley pressed the shutter. Her teeth showed, a smear of white.

Under the collar of her white blouse, there was a silver locket hanging from a thin chain. Haley had never seen her aunt without that locket on.

She zoomed in. The image was unclear, but the chain looked just like the one Haley held in her hand. And she could make out a swirly letter engraved on the locket's surface. A *D*? A *B* for *Brown*? Or was it—

—it was. It was a *P*.

Only the living, Mel had said. Only the living make plots and plans to hurt other people.

A sharp yip from Sunny made Haley jump. The dog hadn't followed Haley into her room. Still staring at the camera, Haley opened the door and leaned out into the hallway. "Hey, Sunny, quit it. Come in."

But Sunny wasn't waiting outside. She was standing near Eddie's room. Her body stiffened; her nose nudged into the crack between the door and door frame. The door swung open.

Sunny growled.

"That's fine for a dog who hid under the bed last night," Haley told her, one eye still on the camera's viewscreen. The silver chain belonged to Aunt Brown. Aunt Brown who never left the house—except that yesterday, she had.

The day after Haley had found the chain on Jake's floor, he'd been sicker than usual. Maia had said he was worse.

Sunny's growl trailed off into a whine.

"Quit it. You'll wake him up." And then the whole house would be in chaos, as usual. Haley needed peace and quiet to think, and that meant she needed Eddie to stay asleep. She walked over to grab Sunny's collar.

Then she hesitated. Last night, somebody had been in Jake's apartment. And Sunny had known.

It couldn't be. Not again.

As quietly as possible, Haley pushed the door open.

Nothing out of the ordinary in the quiet, dim room. Toys scattered across the floor. Shades down. No sound from the crib.

"Sit," Haley told Sunny, low-voiced. "*Stay*."

Sunny whined again, but lowered her hindquarters obediently to the floor.

Careful not to step on anything that would break or squeak, Haley walked the few steps over to the crib. There was Eddie, sleeping faceup, a lump huddled among stuffed giraffes and kittens and the panda bear he had loved almost to shapelessness.

Haley looked down at him. In sleep, his face looked so innocent. All curves, his chubby cheeks and round forehead and the relaxed pout of his lips. It was hard to believe what a little terror he could be when he was awake.

Then Haley's gaze dropped to the little boy's throat.

And she screamed.

CHAPTER SEVENTEEN:
HALEY

Hours later, Haley sat alone on the couch in the living room, hugging her knees close. She didn't even notice the wet, muddy footprints her sneakers were leaving on the yellow cushions.

Her eyes were dry and sore. Every time she blinked, a scene flashed across the inside of her eyelids, lit as if by a strobe light.

Eddie, asleep. Dull red blossoms of blood staining his neck and the folds of the fuzzy white blanket tucked around him.

Elaine's face when she appeared in the doorway of Eddie's room. All the color in her cheeks had drained away; her eyes had looked huge and dark, big enough to swallow up her face. Haley's dad had grabbed at her elbow. Elaine hadn't even put Eddie in the car seat on the way to the hospital. She'd held him on her lap, hugging him, telling him over and over that he would be fine. Her thin, high voice trembled with tears but never quite broke.

The doctor at the emergency room, looking worn-out and tired in his white coat. Haley had to concentrate hard on his words to understand them. Pallor. Weakness. Iron deficiency. Blood tests.

And then her dad's voice, only a little unsteady, but pausing in odd places, as if he could only get out so many words in a row. "My nephew has—has some kind of blood disease. No one's been—able to diagnose it. His mother, my sister, too. Could this be—related?"

"We don't know yet . . . more tests . . . have to wait . . ." The doctor's words blurred in Haley's memory. But her father's voice rang clear.

Oh, yes, she thought. This could be—related.

Her dad and Elaine had sent her home in a taxi. They'd told her to stay by the phone, to ask Mel to come over, that they would call as soon as there was news.

But sitting and waiting weren't things that Haley was planning to do.

She wasn't going to cry, either. And she wouldn't just get angry. She'd *do* something.

Mercy had died. And Edwin. Jake was dying. Not Eddie too, Haley thought grimly. No matter what she had to do, this—*thing*—would not touch her little brother.

Haley's suspicions, worries, fears, beliefs, came tumbling out, half incoherent. Jake simply sat, attentive, frowning a little. The family tree with no dates under Patience's name. The face on her camera's viewscreen, the heartbeat in the graveyard. Aunt Brown walking down the street. Mercy's bloodstained glove. The warning written in the dust. The silver chain.

"We always call her Aunt Brown," Haley finished breathlessly. "But what's her name? Her first name?"

Jake frowned. "I don't know," he said slowly.

"Isn't that weird? And isn't it weird that we call her 'Aunt,' but she's not Dad's sister, not your mom's sister. Is she Granddad's sister?"

"No," Jake answered, even more slowly. "No, Granddad called her Aunt Brown too. I remember."

"But she can't be *his* aunt. That would make her—what? More than a hundred years old? It's just like—she's always been there. Out in that house. All by herself. Isn't it—"

She faltered. Jake picked up the chain from where Haley had put it down on the table by his chair. He wound it around in his fingers. Was he thinking over what she'd said? Or thinking over how he'd break it to her dad and her mom and Elaine that she'd lost her mind?

"And last night, here, I kind of—interrupted. Um. So maybe she—" Jake still wasn't looking at her. "Maybe she needed—you know, more—and Eddie—"

"Eddie. I know. Your dad called from the hospital." Jake rubbed the bandage on his neck. "Haley. I know this is—terrible. What's happening with Eddie. But you can't—"

He had that look on his face.

"—can't make it let you—"

She'd seen that look on Mel's face. On Mr. Samuelson's. On Elaine's. Even on her dad's.

"—think something like this."

But she'd never seen it on Jake's.

"This is crazy. It's not real. It's not what the world really is."

That look of pity. Of smothering sympathy. That look of understanding that didn't understand anything at all.

Haley had never, ever seen Jake look at her like that.

"But what if it's—" How could he do it? Look at her like he knew everything and she knew nothing? "—not like that? Not the way we think?"

If she could just find the right words, he'd change. He'd listen. He'd believe her. He'd be Jake again, the one who was always on her side.

"It's like all those people—no, listen, Jake—who thought the world was flat. If somebody said it was round, they'd call him crazy, right? But it really is. The world is round. What if, what if the world really is—something we think it isn't?"

"Not something like this, Haley."

"Yes, something like this!" Haley knew she shouldn't shout. But she couldn't help it. She wanted to keep her voice calm and even, but it was getting louder all on its own. "I saw that writing in the dust. I *heard* her heart! In the graveyard! Mercy's been trying to tell me—"

"Mercy's *dead*, Haley!"

"Aunt Brown isn't!" Haley had jumped to her feet. "I saw her outside! Look at that chain, Jake. It's real! It's hers! It was *here!*"

Jake let the chain pour out of his fingers into a bright puddle on the tabletop. "Anyone could have dropped that, Haley."

"You're not *listening* to me!"

"Sometimes bad things *happen!*"

Haley stopped, shocked. She never yelled at Jake. Jake never yelled at her.

"You've been fighting really hard not to admit it for a long time," Jake told her as he reached into his pocket. He took out a pack of cigarettes, put one to his lips, and lit it.

You promised you wouldn't. Haley didn't say the words. He knew. He knew what he'd promised.

The cloud of smoke that Jake breathed out coiled and twined in the air.

"But they do; bad things happen even to people you love. Even your own family. I'm sorry, Haley. I'd fix it for you if I could. But making up some crazy story isn't going to help. Bad things just happen."

"The bandage on your neck," Haley said softly.

"What?"

"The bandage. It's bugging you, isn't it? Itching? Take it off."

"Haley, what are you—"

"Just, please . . . take it off."

One corner of Jake's mouth twitched in exasperation. But he tugged a corner of the bandage loose and pulled it away from his skin.

"You can't see the cut," Haley said. "It's gone."

Startled, Jake rubbed his fingers over the smooth, undamaged skin.

"Go look in the mirror."

Frowning, without a word, Jake did so. He left the door to the tiny bathroom open and stared at himself. Haley could see his reflection, along with her own. He looked lost. She looked almost angry.

"You have nosebleeds at night, right, Jake? Blood on your pillow. What if the blood's really from a cut—one that heals really fast? *Unnaturally* fast?"

Jake rubbed the skin on his throat again. With his other hand, the one that still held the cigarette, he clung to the edge of the sink, as if he were afraid of falling.

"And Maia said you have nightmares. Jake, what do you dream about?"

"About—" Jake didn't turn around. In the mirror, his face was even whiter than normal. "Something—holding me down. Crushing me. I can't breathe. Something standing over me, and then—" He stopped.

"And Sunny!" Haley went on, eagerly. Jake was about to believe her, she could tell. He was so close to listening, to understanding. "Sunny went *crazy* last night. Your neighbors say she was barking, right? That's part of why you wanted me to take her. You never heard her, but they said she was barking at night. Right? Jake?"

"No, Haley."

Jake didn't move. He didn't turn around. But he met Haley's eyes in the mirror, and he shook his head.

"Jake!"

"This can't be it. It can't be true. I'm sorry, Haley." He put the cigarette to his mouth with a hand that trembled. He breathed in hard. Smoke came out of his mouth with his next words. "I can handle dying. I'm kind of used to it. But I can't—I just can't think about—something like this."

Haley left him standing there. She shut the apartment door gently behind her and locked it carefully. She knew better than to leave something like that for Jake to do.

He didn't believe her.

She walked stiffly down the hallway, as if her knees didn't quite remember how to bend.

Well. Well, that was—fine. Jake didn't believe her, and that was fine. She'd just have to—

—she'd just have to—

—what would she have to do?

Haley opened the door to the street. A gust of cold wind blew around her. Her jacket was hanging open.

Haley had no idea what to do.

She'd thought Jake would help her. That they'd figure out a plan together.

Now she'd have to do something all on her own. At the thought, cold fear gripped her so tightly that she could barely breathe.

All on her own. Without anybody to help. Without Jake.

Maybe, maybe, maybe Jake was right. Had she made all of this up? Made it up because she was so scared about Jake going away and leaving her that she'd rather believe anything else?

Would she rather go crazy, Haley wondered; would she rather be insane than be alone?

"Haley?"

Haley stared blankly at the battered blue car that had pulled up by the curb. The window rolled down and a concerned face looked out at her.

"What's wrong?" asked Alan O'Neil.

CHAPTER EIGHTEEN:
HALEY

Luckily Elaine liked to cook with a lot of garlic. Haley had one whole clove in her jacket pocket, another for Alan. She'd made the stakes by splitting firewood with her dad's hatchet, whittling them into sharp points with a kitchen knife. The cross she'd gotten at her first communion was around her neck.

She was having a lot of trouble getting used to the idea that Alan O'Neil believed in ghosts.

In other things, too, apparently. In angels and spirits and monsters and everything Jake had just told her was crazy.

And the thing was, he wouldn't stop talking about it.

"I told you about my great-great-uncle, right?"

"Uh. No."

Alan's rattly little car bounced down the street. He had to talk loudly for Haley to hear him over the noise of the engine.

"He dropped dead of a heart attack in the barn one morning. This was back in Ireland. Every morning after that he'd still go out to milk the cows. My great-great-aunt got so used to seeing him, she'd just wave."

"This isn't ghosts."

"Right, right, I know." Alan's fingers tapped on the steering wheel as he drove. "I'm just saying, things happen. All the time. This world, it's weirder than anyone wants to admit. People get all comfortable in their safe little shells and they don't want to even *think* that things could be different. Like your cousin. I mean, he should at least have listened to you, right?"

"It was a crazy story." Haley bristled. "Nobody would have believed it."

Alan looked at her sideways.

"Watch the road!"

He jammed on the brakes for a stop sign. A woman in a green SUV gave them an irritated look as she drove through the intersection.

Haley had no idea why she was being so cold to Alan. She ought to be grateful. He'd been worried enough to stop and pick her up. He'd been patient enough to listen to the whole insane story that, to Haley's disbelief, had come tumbling out of her mouth. And without a moment of hesitation, he'd announced that he was driving her out to her aunt's house so that they could see for themselves. He even had a bulb of garlic in his jacket pocket.

And now he was rattling on about his cousin, who'd worked at a haunted B&B one summer in Providence.

It was just that he was talking so much. It was just that he seemed so excited, as if this were some big adventure.

It was just that he wasn't Jake.

She'd never thought Jake would abandon her. Leave her all on her own.

But she wasn't on her own now, was she? Alan was here, stepping hard on the brakes again as a rusty old pickup truck turned out of the Chestnut Hill Cemetery and onto the road in front of them. And if Haley was a halfway decent person—

which, apparently, she wasn't—she'd be grateful for that. Instead of really, really wishing he would just shut up and let her think.

"And there was this time my brother and me, we were at this vacation house my parents rented, and we heard these footsteps on the floor above. Over and over, you know? And there was nobody in the house but us."

"Yeah?" Haley stared out through the windshield. There was a small backhoe perched on the bed of the pickup truck. A shower of fresh dirt fell from the shovel.

"Only when my dad went up there, he found this squirrel that had gotten in the window, so that probably doesn't count. But still—"

The truck ahead of them picked up speed and Alan stopped talking at last as he turned off the road and had to concentrate on coaxing his car up the steep slope of Aunt Brown's driveway. He stopped and shifted into reverse a couple of times when the wheels spun helplessly in muddy patches. The engine whined as if frustrated and Haley winced at the noise. It wasn't exactly a subtle approach.

But nothing stirred as they got out of the car and climbed the sagging steps of the front porch. The sound of the pickup truck had faded in the distance. There was not enough wind even to send a dry leaf skittering across the grass. Everything was bright, and quiet, and still.

Alan put out a hand to knock on the door. Haley stopped him.

"Let's just—" She hesitated. They'd said they were coming out here to "check" if the story were true. What did that mean, exactly? How did you go about checking to see if somebody was a vampire?

"Let's look around a little, first." Her voice wasn't much above a whisper. She slipped her cell phone out of her pocket and turned it off. The last thing she needed was for that to ring, breaking the silence and letting Aunt Brown know they were poking around in her house.

Alan nodded. He did the same with his phone.

"And thanks," Haley added. She owed him that. "For coming with me."

"Wouldn't miss it," said Alan cheerfully. "Vampire hunting in Exeter, Rhode Island? This'll be the best creepy story ever."

It's not a story; it's my family! Haley wanted to snap at him. But she didn't. Instead, she closed her hand over the doorknob. Even in the sunlight, it felt as cold as if it were coated with frost. She turned it and pushed the door open.

The hallway was exactly as Haley remembered it from her last visit. Sunlight from the door lay in a sheet of light across the floor, blocked by Haley's shadow. Then Alan's shadow joined it. He stood at Haley's shoulder.

Together they stepped into the house.

Chilly and dim. Filtered through shades and curtains, light couldn't fill up the rooms, which loomed like caves, the old-fashioned furniture half lost in shadow.

"Whoa." Alan looked around appreciatively. "Very atmospheric. Very Stephen King."

Everywhere, the familiar earthy smell teased at her nose. Cold and heavy and damp. The smell of wet clay—the smell of the grave. It seemed to cling to the air.

And no one was there.

Hallway, living room, dining room—all were empty. She'd never realized before how *loud* most houses were. A refrigerator humming, a furnace rumbling to life, pipes clanking, a floorboard creaking, a loose window rattling in its frame. None of that here. Haley could hear the air moving in and out of her nose. She could hear Alan breathing at her elbow. She could hear herself swallow.

Alan pushed open a swinging door in the pantry. After a moment his voice broke the silence. Even his low murmur seemed shockingly loud. Haley wanted to scream at him to shut up. She nearly clamped a hand over her own mouth to keep herself from doing it.

"Haley, look."

For a change, he sounded serious.

Haley came to look over his shoulder. The kitchen. A bare wooden table, scrubbed clean, stood in the center of the room. The cupboards were closed, the counters empty.

A cold breeze seemed to wreathe itself around Haley, caressing her neck, whispering down her spine.

"See?"

"See what?" The room looked perfectly normal to Haley. Well, oddly clean, definitely. Even unused. But empty, that was the main point. Where was Aunt Brown?

"There's no refrigerator." Alan took a few steps into the room to open some of the cupboards. Bowls and plates. Cups and saucers. All clean and chilly and white. Haley couldn't help thinking of bones, gnawed clean and stacked tidily away.

Alan turned back to look at Haley. "No food. There's no food anywhere."

Suddenly he didn't seem to think that vampire hunting was so much fun after all. Haley shuddered. Strangely, the bare kitchen seemed more scary than anything else—than the dark figure in Jake's apartment, than the message in the dust, than the heartbeat from the grave. It was so—real. So ordinary. So everyday. So wrong.

"Come on," she insisted. "We have to keep looking."

And what were they going to do if they found something? Haley wondered about that as they climbed the stairs. If they discovered Aunt Brown in an upstairs bedroom or in the attic, what would they do? Say, "Aunt Brown, we think you're a vampire. We think you attacked Eddie. We think you're killing Jake. Come over here so we can stake you"?

Talk about terminal embarrassment.

They'd try to lure her outside, that's what they'd do, Haley decided. Coax her near the front door, the one they'd left open. Pull her outside by force if they had to. There, in the sunlight, they'd see—whatever they'd see. They'd find out if they were both crazy, or if insanity was true.

Haley looked up to the landing and saw the flicker of a gray skirt as it disappeared around the turn in the staircase.

She should have called out, should have shouted, "Aunt Brown!" She should have acted innocent. It would be easier to lure Aunt Brown downstairs, close to the open door, if she acted as if she and Alan had every right to be here.

But she couldn't. The silence in the house crushed the words in her throat.

Instead she ran up to the landing, clutching the newel post to spin herself around. Behind her she heard Alan call, "Haley, wait!"

She stopped, looking up the rest of the stairs to the second-floor hallway. It ran straight ahead from the staircase, three closed doors on the left, three on the right.

And someone standing between them.

Alan nearly ran into Haley. He was gasping for breath. "What're you—"

He didn't finish the sentence.

The stake dropped out of Haley's hand and rolled, bouncing down the stairs. Haley hardly noticed. She found her voice, faint and wavering. "Do you see—her?"

In the half-second that passed between her question and Alan's answer, she had time to think, *Please. Please say yes. Please tell me I'm not alone.*

Alan's voice, low in her ear. "I see her."

134

It wasn't Aunt Brown Haley had glimpsed on the staircase.

A slender, pale young woman, about Haley's height, stood at the top of the stairs. Dark brown hair was pulled into a coil of braids on the back of her head. Heavy bangs framed a face that would have been plain except for the wide, dark eyes. She wore a long gray dress with a full skirt an inch or two off the floor and a small silver locket around her neck.

Only a stray sunbeam or two crept between the curtains of the window at the far end of the hallway, but every detail of the woman's clothes and face was clear, as if she stood in her own light.

And at the same time, Haley could see *through* her. She could make out the hallway behind her, the branching cracks on the bare plaster walls, the panels on the doors.

The woman's mouth moved. She was saying something. Maybe she realized that they couldn't hear her. She repeated herself, despair welling up in those dark eyes, and gestured, reaching out one pale hand and drawing it back toward herself.

That was clear, at least. *Follow me.*

Then she turned aside, so that Haley saw her in profile. Again, she stretched out one hand. This time her wrist twisted as if she were turning a doorknob. She walked through the nearest door and vanished.

Haley was suddenly aware of her heart thumping against her ribs, hard enough, it seemed, to shake her whole body. She felt as if she'd run a marathon standing still.

"That was—" Alan's voice sounded as rattled as she felt. "Um. Unexpected?"

"She wants us to follow her." Haley stared up the staircase at the hallway, the closed door through which the woman had disappeared. Plain, solid wood with a handle of porcelain that had once been white, now dingy gray. It looked exactly the

135

same as the other doors. Nothing to show that someone had just walked through it.

"Yeah. Are we going to?"

The glove, the message on the TV screen, the sound of the heartbeat, the face in Haley's camera. For weeks now, someone had been trying to tell Haley something. Mercy had been trying to tell her something.

Maybe all she had to do was listen.

"We have to," Haley answered Alan. But it still took a determined effort of will for her to lift her foot and set it on the next stair. Clutching the banister tightly, she walked up and into the narrow hallway. If she stretched her arms out, her hands would brush the walls on either side. Alan stayed close behind her.

When they got to the doorway, Haley didn't give herself a second to hesitate. She reached out for the knob, cool and slick beneath her fingers, turned it, and opened the door.

She stepped through it into night.

CHAPTER NINETEEN:
HALEY

There was no shade or curtain on the single window in the room. The sky outside was black, sprinkled with faint stars. And it was icy, as if she'd walked from November into January. There was a single bed against one wall, a rocking chair beside it. A candle in a pewter candlestick sat on the floor, casting a circle of light.

Someone was sitting in the rocking chair, a bright patchwork quilt wrapped around her. It was the woman Haley and Alan had seen in the hall.

Haley whispered her name. "Mercy?"

She couldn't hear her own voice.

And anyway, Mercy was asleep. Her head had fallen back against the chair; her eyes were closed.

She was not the only sleeper in the room.

Someone lay on the bed as well. A quilt sewn in soft browns and grays covered her up to her chin, and the face looked something like Mercy's—the same heavy, dark eyebrows and thick lashes that lay smoothly on her cheeks. But the sleeper's face was thinner than Mercy's, her cheeks pale and sunken, her lips dry and cracked. She looked worn-out and sick.

Haley reached behind her, feeling for Alan, wanting to touch his arm or grab his hand. But her fingers felt nothing but air. She turned. The door was closed behind her; she didn't remember closing it. And Alan wasn't there. Why hadn't he followed her?

Mercy sighed and stirred a little in her chair. The quilt wrapped around her slipped off one shoulder. Haley couldn't help feeling sorry for her. She found herself wanting to step forward and wake her, tell her to go to bed. Tell her that she, Haley, would watch at this sickbed. Because that's surely what Mercy was doing. It must be her sister, lying there ill. Her older sister, Grace, the one who'd died too.

Mercy sighed again. But the figure on the bed didn't stir. Haley stepped closer. Her feet made no sound against the floorboards. There was a light rime of frost on the quilt that covered the sleeper. Haley found herself watching for a breath that would lift the quilt ever so slightly. But none came.

That's when Haley knew. Mercy wasn't watching over a sickbed. She was watching over a deathbed.

Grace had died, quietly, while her sister slept.

Haley felt tears stinging behind her eyes. But why had Mercy brought her here to see this? Haley already knew that Grace had died of the same disease that had killed her mother, would later kill her sister and her brother. What was Mercy trying to tell her by showing her this?

The woman on the bed opened her eyes.

If Haley screamed, she didn't hear the sound. She found herself on the other side of the room, as far from the bed as she could get, without a memory of moving. Grace threw the quilt from her and climbed out of bed. Dark hair slipped from her loose braid to spill around her shoulders. She was wearing only a long sleeveless gown of white linen, trimmed with lace; her feet were bare. The room was freezing, but she didn't seem to notice.

She didn't seem to notice Haley either. Haley might have been invisible. A ghost. Like Mercy.

Had Haley been wrong? Had Grace just been sleeping? But no, Haley was sure that the still figure on the bed had not been breathing. No air stirred in those lungs. No heart pumped blood through veins and arteries beneath that chalky white skin.

Grace smiled slowly. She spread her fingers wide and looked at them closely in the candlelight. She ran her hands slowly up and down her arms and touched her cheeks, her eyelids, her lips, as if her own body were a marvel she had never seen or felt before.

Then she turned to look at her sister, asleep in the rocking chair.

But Grace *died*, Haley's mind insisted, frantic. Grace died and was buried. Her gravestone is right next to Mercy's. Grace can't have—she can't be—this can't be Grace.

Grace hadn't been Mercy's only sister.

Mercy had turned her head a little to one side. Gently, with fingers as pale and light as snowflakes, her sister reached out. She hesitated for a moment. Her hand moved as if she wanted to stroke the soft skin of Mercy's throat. But instead, delicately, she moved aside the locket that hung around her sister's neck.

Haley could see a swirly *M* engraved on the locket's surface.

Grace—no, it wasn't Grace—bent over her sister. As she did so, something slipped loose from the neckline of her shift. A locket swung on its silver chain, identical—except for the *P* engraved on it—to Mercy's.

Grace hadn't been Mercy's only sister. There had been one more. The only one of the four siblings who'd survived. The only one without a tombstone in the cemetery.

Patience.

Maybe she *hadn't* survived. Maybe she'd died, quietly, in the night, with her younger sister watching by her bed. She'd died after all, but no one had known. No one had known because she had refused to stay dead.

Haley saw Patience's mouth open. There were no fangs. A red tongue gently caressed the front teeth, in eagerness.

Mercy stirred a little and whimpered in her sleep. But she didn't wake as her sister bit into her neck. Haley saw the muscles in Patience's throat move as she swallowed.

Haley shouted in terror and outrage. She threw herself forward. And the scene vanished like a reflection in still water when a stone is thrown in.

The candlelight was gone. Darkness closed over Haley's head, bringing with it a foul smell. Sound burst over her. Someone was kicking a door, yanking the doorknob, rattling the wood in its frame. And shouting.

"Haley! Are you okay? Are you in there? *Answer* me!"

"Okay!" Haley shouted back. She ran to the door. It was latched on the inside. How could that have happened? She flipped the latch up and Alan almost fell into the room. He grabbed Haley's arm.

"Are you all right? What happened?"

"Mercy. She showed me. I know who she is. She's—"

"That woman was there, I saw her, and then you—I swear, Haley, you went *through* the door after her and I couldn't open it—"

"Mercy's sister. Patience. She died—I mean, she didn't—I mean, she's still—"

"That *smell*. What's that smell?"

Haley and Alan both stopped talking and took stock of where they were.

"This was Patience's room," Haley said slowly, looking around. "Mercy's sister. The older one." The room was nearly as dark as it had been in Mercy's time, with no candle burning to lighten the blackness. Haley groped her way to the window and pulled the heavy curtains aside.

The room hadn't changed. The bed still stood by the wall, the rocking chair near its head. Both were empty.

On an old dresser near the window, there was a hairbrush, a comb, and a small silver locket without its chain, an elaborate *P* engraved on its surface.

The smell seemed strongest by the bed. Swallowing hard, Haley walked toward it. The dull brown quilt that had covered Patience's body was gone, replaced by a plain blanket of iron-gray wool.

Reluctantly, her fingers twitching, Haley reached out to touch the blanket. She pulled it back.

Stains covered the sheets beneath and splotched the pillow-case. Most were old and brown, a few rusty red.

The stench rose up and hit Haley in the face. It was like a living thing, trying to smother her. She dropped the blanket. Her stomach heaved.

Then Alan grabbed her arm and pulled her back, out into the hall, and slammed the door behind them.

"Come on, Haley. Let's go."

"We can't! We have to—"

"We have to *leave*." Alan was still holding her arm, so hard it hurt. "This is crazy, this is dangerous, and we have to get out of here."

"You knew it was dangerous before!" Haley protested. "You said you wouldn't miss it!"

"Yeah, well, now it's dangerous *and* real," Alan said flatly. And Haley knew he was right.

They had stakes and garlic and crosses. All that stuff that worked in the movies. But now, after seeing what Mercy had shown her—that avid hunger in Patience's eyes, that cool eagerness with which she'd turned down her sister's collar and moved aside that lock of hair—Haley knew she didn't want to face the vampire. She didn't want to see her. Ever.

Haley didn't care if Alan was a coward. She didn't care if she was one too. She nodded to show him she agreed.

But he wasn't looking at her. He was staring over her shoulder, looking at the staircase down the hall.

"What?"

"Your friend's here again."

His hand on her arm turned her around.

Mercy was standing at the top of the stairs, that same look of urgency in her eyes. She gestured again, drawing her hand toward herself. *Follow me.*

The she turned and walked quickly down the stairs. Haley distinctly saw her gray skirt swirl through the rods of the banister.

Haley was still staring after her when she heard a soft footstep close behind her. She turned just in time to see Aunt Brown put out a thin, frail hand and push Alan down the stairs.

Haley simply stood and watched him fall. She was stuck, trapped, her muscles frozen, her bones turned to stone. She was appalled at how long it took him to fall. At how still he lay when he'd reached the bottom.

Aunt Brown glanced at Alan's unmoving body and then shifted her disapproving gaze to Haley. "Children today have no manners at all," she said. "It is extremely rude to enter a house uninvited."

Haley wrenched herself into motion and scrambled down the stairs. Alan was sprawled faceup across the faded carpet. His eyes were closed, but Haley couldn't see any blood. He was breathing.

She looked up. Aunt Brown was coming slowly down the stairs.

Haley was pretty sure you weren't supposed to move someone after a fall. Concussion. Broken back. Paralysis.

She was also pretty sure you weren't supposed to leave someone in the path of a hungry vampire.

She grabbed at the shoulder of Alan's jacket and heaved. His body moved a few inches before her hand slipped free. She flopped back and sat down hard.

Aunt Brown stepped off the staircase and onto the floor of the hallway.

"Stay away," Haley said. Her voice was thin and weak and quavering. She didn't sound brave at all.

Well, she wasn't.

"Don't hurt him." She tried again. "Don't you hurt him, or I'll—"

"He does not matter." Aunt Brown stepped over Alan as if he were a pile of trash. "But you should not have brought him here."

She stood looking down at Haley.

"He is not *family*," Aunt Brown said. "Family is what matters."

Then Haley heard it. The whine of tires spinning in gravel. The growl of a car engine trying to climb a steep hill.

Someone was coming. Someone who would help! Haley saw her stake lying on the carpet and snatched it up, stuffing it in her pocket as she scrambled to her feet. She threw herself out the door just as a silver car skidded to a stop beside Alan's.

The door opened and Jake got out.

Haley knew she was babbling and couldn't help herself. Words were tumbling out, that it was true, it was all true, and she was in there, and Alan was hurt. Jake was looking at her as if she were crazy, which was exactly how she sounded.

"Wait," he said. "Haley, *wait*."

He was breathing heavily, and leaned against the car. And Haley remembered that Jake wasn't supposed to drive anymore. "Your dad called me, said you weren't answering your cell or at home," he went on. "I thought you might be out here. I can't believe you really—"

But Haley couldn't wait for him to finish. "He's hurt, Jake, she hurt him." She grabbed at her cousin's arm and felt how thin it was, the bones right under the skin. Disloyally, ungratefully, she wished someone else had come to rescue her, somebody who would be more use in a fight. "We have to get out of—I mean, we have to help him—I mean—"

"Aunt Brown?"

There came the quiet, definite thud of a door closing, and the metallic snick of a latch clicking into place. Haley spun around to see Aunt Brown standing on the porch.

"Haley's very upset," Jake said calmly to Aunt Brown. "I've come to take her home."

CHAPTER TWENTY:
HALEY

Aunt Brown didn't answer Jake. She set a foot on the first of the porch steps.

"It's all right," Haley said to Jake. "She can't come down; it's all right."

"*What* are you talking about?"

"Just watch. The sunlight. She can't go out into the sunlight."

In a few seconds, Jake would see. He'd have to admit that he had been wrong, and she'd been right.

Aunt Brown stepped off of the stairs and walked calmly across the dry, withered grass. Nothing—not her calm face, her steady gait, her disapproving eyes—changed as the sunlight fell over her.

Jake let out his breath in an irritated sound that was half snort, half sigh.

"Okay. Now can you see that you made all of this up?" he asked as Aunt Brown walked closer.

"But she—but she—" *Could* Jake be right? Was Aunt Brown really—not what Mercy had shown her? But whatever she was, she'd hurt Alan. She could have killed him. "Jake, she—"

Aunt Brown had come to a stop in front of them. She looked thoughtfully at Jake. Then she drew her arm back and hit him.

As thin as Jake was, he was still taller and heavier than Aunt Brown. Her slap shouldn't have done more than turn his head on his neck. It certainly shouldn't have flung him to the ground ten feet away.

Haley stared, appalled, at Jake as he struggled to rise to his hands and knees. Blood dripped from his nose. That was impossible, it couldn't have happened, it didn't—

Before she could break through her shock, she saw Aunt Brown lift her hand to her mouth. There was a smear of red across her knuckles. She licked it delicately as she raised her eyes to meet Haley's.

Haley felt as if a bucket of ice water had been poured over her head. She stumbled back a step, shoving both hands in the pockets of her jacket, searching. She'd put the stake in there, she had it—

Aunt Brown was right in front of her now. Haley had barely seen her move. As Haley's left hand, clutching something, came out of her pocket, Aunt Brown's fingers clamped around hers.

Cold. The fingers touching Haley's were as icy as bare metal on a winter day. Was it possible that Haley had never touched her aunt before? Not a kiss on the cheek, not a handshake, not a brush of fingertips? It must be. Because if she had ever felt this before, this cold that was freezing her hand, creeping past her wrist and up her arm, she'd have remembered. She'd have known.

It wasn't the stake in her hand after all. It was the clove of garlic. Aunt Brown's fingers tightened over Haley's. The juice of the raw garlic began to drip through Haley's fingers.

"That won't work," Aunt Brown said—*Patience, think of her as Patience*, Haley thought wildly. *Think of her as Patience, not your aunt. It will be easier.* "Foolish foreign superstition." Patience tightened her grip a little. "Nothing to do with what I am."

Patience's eyes were as cold as her fingers, her voice even and calm, and Haley couldn't move. Couldn't speak. Couldn't think. Could barely breathe. Was this the feeling that had trapped Mercy and Jake, both asleep, unable to wake, unable to resist, as the vampire's teeth met the soft flesh of their throats?

"Hunger drives every living thing," Patience said reasonably. "Animals hunt. Even plants fight for soil and light. Life is hunger. Why shouldn't I take life to feed my own?"

Because you had a life, Haley thought. Her jaws were locked, incapable of forming words, but her mind still functioned. *Now you're taking other people's. Mercy's. Jake's. Eddie's.*

"They tried to leave me in the cold," Patience said, as if she'd heard Haley thinking the names of her family. "They said they loved me, but they would have abandoned me. Piled earth over me and left me to rot. If I'd let them. If I'd stayed—"

Dead. Patience wouldn't say the word *dead.*

Haley wrenched at her arm, but it was like pulling against a steel bolt. She'd have to break her hand off at the wrist to be free.

"You understand." Patience's arm bent at the elbow. Slowly, she was pulling Haley closer. "It's what you want yourself. You can have it if you choose. No more grief. No more loss. Nothing changes."

That's not—that's not what I wanted! But the thought wasn't true. Haley had wished for that, longed for it. Somehow, Patience had known.

"I told you." Patience's voice was as chilly and smooth and gray as polished steel. "We are an old family. And this is in us. We have the will to choose life. The strength to go on. You merely . . ." She hesitated, as if it were hard to find words for something so simple. "*Make a choice.*" She whispered it. "When that cold comes, you turn away from it. You take what you want. You take *life*."

From others, Haley thought. *You take life from others.* Was that what Patience was telling her? *If I want life badly enough to steal it from the people I love most—then I never have to die?*

"You are the first I've seen whose desire is strong enough. I have felt it in you. You want what I wanted. For life to go on. Forever."

Cold. That hand was so cold on her wrist. Those words were so cold in her mind.

"And you can have what you want so much. It is simply— the choice to live."

Incredibly, Patience smiled. Gently, tenderly.

"Then we could be together. Family."

Something crashed into both of them. Haley hit the ground hard, and the icy grip on her hand was broken. Her hair was flung into her eyes; she couldn't see; something was on her, a heavy pressure; an angry snarl rang in her ears; a hand snatched at her face—

Someone dragged her up and shoved her forward. "Car!" Jake yelled. He was the one who'd shoved them both down, Haley realized; he was the one who'd broken Patience's hold on her. Then she thought of nothing but running. She fell against Jake's car, the metal of the door handle slick under her fingers. Sobbing, she wrenched at it, the door swung wide, and she threw herself into the passenger seat, slamming the door after her.

Jake was beside her, blood dripping down his face. He jerked the gearshift into neutral so that the car began rolling down the hill even before he jammed the keys into the ignition.

"Alan," Haley gasped. "Jake, we can't leave Alan!"

"Who's Alan?"

Something thudded against the car door on Haley's side. Patience's fingers scrabbled at the window. But then the engine caught and Jake stamped on the gas. Gravel shot from under the wheels and Jake's door swung wildly—he hadn't taken a second to close it—as the car tore down the driveway.

Haley heard her own shriek echoing in her ears. She hadn't even been aware of yelling.

Gripping the steering wheel with one hand, Jake reached out with the other to snag the door on his side and swing it shut before returning both hands to the wheel and braking a little to make the turn out onto the highway.

"Jake, listen!" Haley insisted. "We have to go back for—"

Then the glass in Jake's window exploded.

In the half-second before the car swerved wildly, Haley's mind saw the picture. *Click.* The arm thrusting through the broken glass to grab at Jake's shoulder. The glass didn't shatter; it crumbled into glittering gravel. One sharp edge sliced through cloth and skin into muscle, but no blood flowed. The arm reaching into the car was dead flesh.

Then the car swung toward the ditch on the side of the road and the dashboard came flying up at Haley's face.

Haley woke up a little bit at a time. She was huddled uncomfortably, her knees tucked up near her chest, one arm twisted under her. She tried to turn, to stretch, but there was no room. How had her bed cramped around her like this, holding her like a nut in its shell? Her head throbbed and her lower lip stung. A taste that was thin and salty was leaking into her mouth.

With an effort, Haley opened her eyes. She needed to figure things out. There was something dark green and fuzzy inches from her nose. Bits of gravel and dirt were stuck in it, and tiny sparkling pieces of broken glass. Haley blinked hard and things came into focus. Carpet. She was lying on carpet, packed into a small, dark, curved space.

Then Haley got it. She was in Jake's car, lying scrunched up in the space under the dashboard. She must have fallen down there after she hit her head—

Jake's car. Jake!

Twisting, crawling, scrambling, Haley fought her way back up onto the passenger seat. Through the cracked windshield she could see nothing but old, yellowed grass. The horizon through the side window was slanted crazily, making her stomach swoop dizzily. She thought for a second that something was wrong with her eyes, but then she realized that the car itself had tipped, nose down, into the ditch alongside the road. The keys were still in the ignition. No sign of Jake.

The window on the driver's side had been shattered. Fragments of glass, icy white, were scattered across the seat.

Haley could get her door open, but no more than a few inches. The window wouldn't go down. She ended up crawling out of the broken window on the driver's side, pulling the sleeves of her jacket down over her hands to protect them, shielding her face with her arms.

On hands and knees, slipping in cold mud, she tried to climb out of the ditch. She slid back once, and one foot ended up ankle-deep in icy cold, slimy water. Shivering, grabbing handfuls of long grass, she heaved herself up beside the road and stood for a moment to catch her breath.

Her whole body ached, a vague throbbing that sharpened most keenly in the arm that had been twisted under her, the lip she'd cut against her teeth, and a spot over her right eyebrow.

Putting up cautious fingers, she encountered a lump too tender to touch. But everything worked. Right now that was enough.

To her right, behind the wrought-iron fence, was the cemetery. To her left, past the ditch, was the road. Not a car in sight.

Haley had no idea how long she'd been unconscious. A few minutes? An hour? More? Not long enough for someone to see the wrecked car and stop.

With stiff, cold fingers she clawed her cell phone out of her pocket. Just three little numbers, just 9-1-1, and she'd have help. Police, ambulance. *People*, lots of them, so she wouldn't be facing this nightmare by herself.

Her phone slipped out of her clumsy fingers, cartwheeled in the air, and vanished with a sickening *plop* into the icy puddle at the bottom of the ditch.

Without a second thought, Haley threw herself down after it.

She ended up on her knees, icy water soaking through her jeans. The puddle was murky brown; she couldn't see a thing. Groping frantically, she clawed through slimy grass and slick mud, trying hard not to think about what she might be touching. Her hands were so cold they hurt; she could have cried from the pain. And the smell of wet clay was choking her. It was worse than being inside Aunt Brown's house. It was as bad as being at the bottom of a grave.

There. She felt it. The hard, smooth rectangle of her phone. She hauled it out, flipped it open, brushed the slimy mud away. She tried to turn it on. Nothing. She shook it. She rubbed it dry on her jacket.

Nothing. Of course, nothing. It would never work after falling into that filthy water.

Haley stuffed the dead phone in her pocket and climbed out of the ditch for the second time.

Now she really was all alone.

She could run along the road, wave down a car, find a house. But what about Jake? What about Alan? By the time she found some help, it could be too late for both of them.

Still, what could Haley do, all on her own?

There weren't even any helpful strangers coming along the road. There was no one to do this with her. And she didn't have time to let that scare her. She had to make a choice.

Blowing on her cold hands, Haley looked at the cemetery. It was empty. She looked across the road, up the graveled drive-way, to the shabby old farmhouse.

Alan was probably still there. And would Patience have taken Jake back there as well? She was strong, stronger than Haley had imagined. Haley felt a shudder crawl over her, remembering how easily the frail old woman had struck Jake and knocked him aside.

The thought of stepping back into that quiet, dim house made Haley's throat close up with terror. But Patience had lived there for—what? More than a hundred years now? It seemed likely she'd retreat there if threatened or attacked.

Haley took a deep breath, let it out slowly, and prepared to scramble down into the ditch again for a third time and up the other side when something brushed her arm. Light as a feather, as a breath of wind.

She turned her head and saw nothing.

She had to go.

That touch a second time. And something flickering at the corner of her vision.

Haley looked again.

It was hard to see Mercy. One moment she was there, the next she wasn't. Haley remembered how surprised she'd been the first time she'd seen a fire in the daylight. At night the orange flames looked nearly solid. In the sunlight they were close to transparent. Hardly there.

Mercy was like that. Haley had to squint and move her head to see her. That urgent face, that gesture with her hand. *Follow me.*

Mercy turned. She walked easily through the fence, as if it wasn't there. Maybe for her it wasn't.

Alan had said that Haley, following Mercy, had walked right through a door. But that didn't happen this time. When she put a hand on the fence, it was solid.

"Wait," she called to Mercy. "I can't just walk through stuff, you know."

Mercy, a vague gray figure, wavering a little with the wind, seemed to pause. Haley clutched the cold iron rails, hauled herself up the fence—

—and jumped down on the other side into the past.

CHAPTER TWENTY-ONE:
HALEY

The cemetery had shrunk around her. Less than half as big, it huddled close to the road. The fence was gone, replaced by a low stone wall. The grass was neatly mown, the headstones straight. The sunlight had vanished. Thick, low gray clouds covered the sky.

Less than a hundred yards away, four men were carrying a coffin. They were dressed in dark suits, hats on their heads. A line of people came behind them. The women all wore long, old-fashioned dresses, like Mercy's. Some had shawls around their shoulders and heads.

No, Haley thought. *No, Mercy, I can't be here. I have to find Jake—*

But Mercy wasn't there.

Haley looked around in panic. There was no figure at her side, flickering at the edge of her vision. And Mercy wasn't among the women walking behind the coffin, either.

Had Mercy brought her here and abandoned her? Left her a hundred years in the past, away from Patience—and Alan, and Jake?

"Mercy!" she shouted. Or meant to. Her voice made no sound. She grabbed at a nearby headstone and felt nothing. Her fingertips moved through the solid stone as easily as through mist.

A ghost. She was a ghost.

With nothing else to do, Haley ran toward the funeral. She had seen Mercy, when Mercy was a ghost in Haley's time. Maybe somebody now—then—would see her, help her.

The men were carrying the coffin toward a place Haley remembered. They hadn't reached it yet, but Haley could see where they were headed. A willow tree—not as tall as the last time Haley had seen it—leaned near a cluster of gravestones. A man stood near it with a shovel in his hand, waiting patiently for the mourners to reach him. At his feet was a trim, straight-sided hole in the ground. A small hole, to fit a small coffin. Edwin's coffin.

Haley had reached the pallbearers by now as they continued their slow march across the cemetery. One of the men carrying the coffin was staring straight ahead, his jaw clenched. He looked furious. Tears were running almost invisibly down his face and creeping into a thick black beard.

"Hey!" Haley shouted uselessly. "I'm here!" She waved her arms. "Can you hear me? Can you see me?"

The weeping man didn't turn his head. But one of the women walking behind the coffin glanced up. Smooth, dark hair was pulled into a braided knot on the back of her head. Her dress and shawl were black, her face pale, her cheeks brushed with red from a chilly wind. There were no tears in her eyes.

Haley had last seen her barefoot, in a long white shift, bending over her sleeping sister.

Patience.

Haley flinched as Patience seemed to look straight at her. Suddenly she no longer wanted to draw attention to herself. She backed away quickly, stumbling, walking through headstones because she didn't dare turn, didn't dare take her eyes off Patience, who was still looking around, frowning a little, as if she'd heard something she couldn't quite catch.

Then a flicker at the corner of her eye caught Haley's attention. Something had moved. Had it been the man, leaning on his shovel near the newly dug grave? But as her head turned toward him, he disappeared.

The funeral, the coffin, the mourners vanished as well.

But Patience was still there.

Jake was sprawled on his back near Mercy's grave. His head was turned toward Haley, his eyes closed. There was blood on his throat, running down his neck, soaking into the collar of his white shirt.

He didn't move or stir as Patience, crouched over him, lifted her head. There was a smear of blood on her lower lip. Slowly she licked it away.

Haley shuddered, but she didn't back up. Her mind shouted, *Run!* It shouted, *Help him! Save him! He saved you!* The commands clashed and tangled along her nerves; her feet stayed rooted.

Gracefully, Patience rose to her feet, smoothing out her skirt. She still looked like the Aunt Brown Haley had known all her life, but something was different. She seemed younger. Her cheeks were flushed red. Even her hair, slipping loose from its knot, looked a little darker. She didn't look thin and frail anymore. She looked . . . strong.

Run. Get away.

But Jake didn't move, didn't open his eyes. Was he breathing? She couldn't tell.

Patience smiled, just a little. Was it a smile? Her upper lip lifted, showing her teeth. No fangs. They were just ordinary teeth, sharp and white and—

This was a predator with hunger in her eyes. Haley wasn't
family to her now. Wasn't even a person. She was simply prey.

Like any hunted animal, Haley turned and ran.

She felt something snag the collar of her jacket, something
sharp graze the back of her neck. But Patience had tried too
soon; she wasn't quite close enough to get the grip she needed.
Haley dodged, dove aside between a row of headstones, heard a
snarl of frustrated rage behind her.

Haley's mind shut off. She wasn't thinking, just running. The
urge filled up her head, not even a word, just a command—*faster
faster faster.*

Fear flicked at her like the lash of a whip. *She's behind you—
she'll catch you—you'll die. You'll be dead. Like Jake.*

She didn't dare to look over her shoulder, couldn't hear
anything but the rasp of her own breath. But Patience must
surely be right behind her. She'd outrun a car. Haley's mind
flinched from that thought. But it was true. Patience had caught
up with the car, had dragged Jake from it. How was Haley going
to escape from something like that?

Haley saw a crypt up ahead, a small square building of white
marble blotched with lichen, and she ducked around its corner.
She hesitated a moment, her back against the wall. Patience
would be after her any second. But then Haley would know
where the vampire was. Haley would get the crypt in between
them, she thought. Then she'd run for the road and pray for a
car to stop. It wasn't much of a plan, but between terror and
exhaustion, it was all she had.

Except that Patience didn't appear.

Silence. The sunlight shone on quiet rows of gravestones.
No wind stirred the grass or the twigs of the leafless trees. No
birds, no squirrels. Haley's breath had settled down to deep,
slow gasps. But even without that dreadful rasping in her ears,
she couldn't hear a thing.

She turned her head slowly, scanning the graveyard. Nothing moved.

Then she understood.

She wasn't just being hunted. She was being stalked.

Patience was hiding somewhere, watching. Waiting for Haley to make the first move. Waiting to have her out in the open, with nowhere to hide.

It was hopeless. The minute Haley moved away from the shelter of the crypt, Patience would spring out from wherever she was concealed. And Haley would be dead. Dead like Jake.

Or worse. *You want what I wanted*, Patience had told Haley. *You must simply make a choice.*

A choice. Haley clung to the memory of those words. So if Haley didn't choose, she didn't have to be—what Patience was?

But would she do it? At the moment of death, with her blood draining away, would she choose to let go? Or would she hold onto life with all her strength? Would she demand to go on living, even if she lived as nothing but hunger?

Haley didn't want to be forced to make that choice.

She looked over the graveyard again, hoping for something—some sign, some movement, some hint. But Patience was too smart to give herself away. She was good at waiting, and at hiding. She'd had more than a century of practice.

When Haley turned her head back to the left, someone was standing beside her.

Haley flinched, thumping into the cool stone wall at her back. Mercy looked at her sorrowfully. But this time Haley wasn't fooled.

It was Mercy who'd lured her into the graveyard, far from help. It was Mercy who had distracted her at the top of the stairs, letting Patience approach and push Alan down.

Haley shook her head angrily as Mercy reached out a hand. Ghosts and vampires. She'd been crazy to trust one and not the other.

"You got what you wanted," Haley said between her teeth, whispering angrily. "What, you were lonely? You wanted more victims to keep you company?"

Mercy only looked sadder. Her hand stayed out, beseechingly. The silver locket around her neck caught the light in a flash of brightness.

Haley moved a few inches away, but Mercy stayed next to her, although Haley couldn't see how, exactly, she moved. Her hand touched the front of Haley's red jacket.

Mercy frowned, as if she were concentrating hard. And Haley's jacket actually moved, as if ruffled by a cold little breeze.

Haley rubbed the jacket's collar between two fingers, confused. "This? What?"

Mercy gestured, her fingers fluttering. *Give it to me.*

Another trap? Another trick?

But how? What kind of a trap could involve Haley's jacket?

Please. The urgency on Mercy's face didn't need words.

Why would she want this so badly? She didn't need to trick Haley now, to lead her anywhere. Haley was in the graveyard already, easy prey for the vampire. Nothing Mercy could do would make things worse.

And she was pleading.

Slowly Haley slipped the jacket off her shoulders and held it out. Mercy reached to take it. Or tried to. The thick fleece trembled as her hands passed through it.

Haley shook her head. "You can't—"

And yet, Mercy had written that message in the dust of the TV screen, Haley remembered. She *could* touch things, move things, if she wanted to.

But dust weighed close to nothing. The jacket had to be a pound, maybe two.

Mercy tried again. This time Haley actually felt the weight of the jacket lift for a few seconds. Mercy was trembling with the effort. Then the coat sagged back into Haley's hands.

Whatever Mercy's plan was, it wasn't going to work.

Mercy turned her back on Haley. For a moment Haley expected her to vanish, but she simply stood there, waiting.

Then Haley understood. She put the jacket gently over Mercy's shoulders. Holding her breath, she took her hands away very slowly.

Mercy slumped as though Haley had laid a lead blanket over her back. Her image wavered for a moment, like candle flame flickering in a gust of wind. But then her figure steadied, became stronger, and she straightened. Against her dull gray skirt and dark hair, Haley's jacket seemed to glow, bright as holly berries against deep green leaves. Bright as fresh blood.

Without turning, Mercy gestured again. *Follow me.*

Mercy ran across the grass, dodging between gravestones, quicker than Haley could ever have been. And something was after her. Something leapt off the roof of the crypt—*She was hiding up there there the whole time?* Haley thought, appalled—and was instantly on Mercy's trail. Nothing human could run that quickly, could turn that lightly. Feral, Patience hunted her sister, hungry for blood.

But Haley noticed something. Mercy ran lightly across the graves, blades of grass never bending under her feet. But Patience stayed on the paths of trodden earth between the headstones. She wouldn't set foot on a grave. That let Mercy, even weighed down by the burden of Haley's jacket, keep just ahead of her, as she led Patience back toward the Brown family plot.

The path between Haley and the cemetery gate was clear now. But Mercy had told her to follow.

And Jake. Mercy was leading Patience back toward Jake. Or his body.

All this took only a few seconds of panicked thought, before Haley spat out the worse curse she knew, thrust her hand in her pocket, feeling for the stake she'd put there, and ran after Mercy and Patience.

Mercy, leading her sister, twisted and dodged. Haley, running in a straight line, gained on them. *Running toward a vampire, I'm crazy, oh God please—*

She barely noticed the scene change around her. The cemetery shrank, the wrought-iron fence vanished. The road outside lost its paving. The distant murmur of traffic vanished. Even the light altered as clouds suddenly blotted out the sun. But Haley didn't care. Not even the mourners now drawing close to the grave surprised her enough to slow her down. None of them stared or looked up at this madness, this frantic race interrupting their funeral. Not even the gravedigger under the willow turned his head to look.

Mercy, in Haley's red jacket, led her sister past their brother's open grave. Haley followed. And then the scene flickered and changed again. A thin rain was falling, although Haley could not feel it, and she was running past a teenage boy, his face shocked and miserable, a tie knotted close around his neck, a suit jacket engulfing his skinny shoulders.

He didn't see her, didn't know her. But she knew him. Jake.

And she knew the people behind him, too. She saw her father, his arm around her mom—not Elaine, her mom. She saw herself, like an old picture come to life, solemn and scared, clinging to her mom's hand, staring at Jake, waiting for him to notice her.

Haley remembered. Aunt Nell's funeral. She hadn't really understood that it was her aunt in the coffin, hadn't really understood that Aunt Nell would never come back. All she'd really understood was that, for the first time ever, Jake wouldn't look at her.

But she couldn't stop for the memory, couldn't reach out to Jake, couldn't comfort her little-girl self. She was still running, Mercy was still leading her, and Patience too, deeper into the cemetery, in and out of the past.

Mercy stopped, her back to Haley and Patience. The rain stopped too. An airplane roared overhead. They were back in the present once more.

Something crunched under Haley's feet as she came to a halt. She glanced down and saw birdseed scattered over the grass.

Haley choked out a warning as Patience closed in on her sister, reaching out, and Mercy just stood there, motionless.

Then Mercy disappeared.

The red jacket fluttered down. Patience snatched at it and snarled. Her back was to Haley, but any second she would turn, and this time there was no point in even trying to run. Haley knew she would not be fast enough. She knew she had no chance.

Then something flickered into being behind Patience, between Haley and the vampire. First a shimmer in the air, as if the light were folding in on itself. Then a ripple of darkness. Mercy appeared. But she wasn't alone.

There was something, someone, at her side. A boy, dressed in heavy boots, a dark gray suit, a cap on his short, fair hair. And on Mercy's other side, a slender figure in a leaf-green dress. Hair so blond it was almost white blew and rippled in a wind that didn't touch Haley.

Patience turned.

163

She flinched and took a step backward. Then she was falling.

For the first time, Haley saw an emotion that wasn't hunger on her aunt's face.

It was terror. Patience fought not to fall, but the grave had her. She was gone.

Panting, shivering, Haley clutched the stake tightly and waited, staring at the black hole into which Patience had disappeared. The grave was so fresh that she could smell the damp soil. The orange nylon rope that she had seen before was gone. Soon there would be a funeral, and someone would rest in that grave. There would be a headstone, and a coffin. But for now there was nothing but a neat, square pit in the ground.

Patience would crawl back out of it in a minute. It was just a short fall. It wouldn't really hurt her. Nothing could hurt her. She was already dead.

Edwin turned to look at Haley, a little boy with solemn eyes. And the fair-haired woman in the green dress turned too. Haley let the stake fall out of her hand.

"Aunt Nell?" she whispered.

That's why Mercy had led her into the past, back to the funerals for two of Patience's victims. She'd brought them back, somehow, Haley thought. She'd brought them with her.

Aunt Nell tucked a strand of hair behind her ear, smiled, flickered, and vanished. But Mercy and Edwin remained.

Mercy put one arm around Edwin's shoulder and gestured at the grave. *Come look.*

Haley picked up the stake again. Cautiously, she edged closer.

Patience didn't leap out of the hole to drag her down. Haley peered into the grave.

Dust. Bones, half eaten away by time. Haley saw the curve of a skull, the long lines of femurs and tibia. Not ivory white. Brown with age.

The grave Patience had tried so hard to avoid for a century had taken what it was owed.

Did something stir in the bones and ashes? Haley reluctantly looked again.

There, in what remained of the cage made by the ribs, something twitched. Horrified, Haley knelt to look closer. Something that wasn't brown with age, that wasn't dust or earth or bone, something dark red throbbed slightly, steadily.

Patience's heart still beat.

Mercy knelt beside her. She nodded at Haley. At the stake in Haley's hand.

"No," Haley whispered. "I can't. No!"

Mercy simply looked at her. This time she didn't need to gesture to make Haley understand. *Your turn now.*

Gritting her teeth, trying not to breathe, Haley climbed down into the grave. The earth walls closed her in. The rectangle of cloudy sky overhead seemed miles away. When she couldn't avoid inhaling any longer, the scent of clay clogged her nostrils and clotted in her throat.

Half the skull had crumbled away. One black, empty eye socket watched Haley, almost beseechingly. She rolled the stake in her palm, the wood dry and splintery. She tested the point with a finger.

Patience had wanted life so badly. She was harmless now, surely. Would it be so bad to let her go on, not to snuff out this last faint claim to life?

(You understand. You want what I wanted. I know it.)

Haley thought of the grave being filled in. Clods of dirt falling, heavy and thick. And beneath them, the heart still beating, still alive.

As long as there's blood in the heart, Haley remembered. That's what they had believed, Mercy's friends and family. As long as there was fresh blood in the heart, the dead body wasn't dead. It was living off someone else.

They'd had the wrong sister, but they hadn't been wrong. They'd known.

Haley thought of Jake. Of Eddie. She couldn't risk it.

She lifted the stake and brought it down.

When Haley had dragged herself out of the grave, digging her toes into the soft earth and clutching at the grass with her fingers, Mercy and Edwin were gone. Her red jacket lay in the grass at her feet.

She stood gasping for a moment, and then began to run.

Jake was lying near Mercy's grave. He was perfectly still, blood thick on his throat, his face chalky white.

Haley threw herself down beside him, fumbling to find a pulse on the undamaged side of his neck. Where did you look for a pulse anyway? Her fingers were shaking and cold, but his skin was colder and slick with blood. She couldn't feel a thing.

Chapter Twenty-Two:
HALEY

The sunlight fell gently over the white and gray head-stones. It was a chilly light with no warmth in it, but it had brightness.

The breeze was cold, too. Haley had left her bike by the cemetery gate and now she zipped up her coat to her neck. That morning she'd left her red fleece jacket in the closet and pulled out a down parka instead. She had to admit it: Winter was coming. Not today, not tomorrow, but soon. The graveyard would be covered in thick white, like a quilt tucked over a bed. It would look protected and safe.

Maybe she'd come back to take some more pictures, Haley thought. Seasons in the Chestnut Hill Cemetery. That would look interesting in her portfolio for art school.

Haley tucked her hands into her pockets and walked briskly. She didn't have much time.

The cemetery stayed reassuringly normal around her. The wrought-iron fence didn't shift in and out of existence. There was no one carrying a small coffin toward an open grave, no teenage boy with a stricken face and a suit jacket that was too big. Wind rustled the grass and swished through the bare twigs.

High overhead, in the branches of the willow that bent over the Brown plot, a squirrel chattered angrily as Haley walked underneath.

Mercy's grave looked as it had a few weeks ago, when Haley had come here with Mel to take pictures for her history project. The stone was tilted just a bit to one side. Haley wished she could straighten it. Kneeling down, she settled for rubbing some lichen away from the carved letters of Mercy's name.

Haley felt like she should sense something, kneeling there. Some connection with Mercy, some emotion, a whisper in her ear—*Well done*, perhaps. But the only thing she could feel was the cold, smooth stone under her fingertips and the damp earth soaking through the knees of her jeans.

She remembered the scrambling horror of that day, her utter inability to decide what to do. Should she stay with Jake? Should she run for help? Should she press on the wound in his throat to stop the bleeding or would that hurt his breathing? But she'd run at last, out into the road, flagging down a passing driver and nearly getting killed herself, not that she'd noticed at the time. Then getting in the ambulance with Jake.

She'd been about to send the ambulance back for Alan when he arrived on his own. He'd come to in Aunt Brown's empty house and stumbled out to the road, where a passerby had picked him up and brought him to the emergency room.

After that the memory was a blur of tiredness and worry and questions that Haley had answered clumsily—she'd thought she should tell Aunt Brown about Eddie, Alan had offered to take her, he'd fallen down the stairs, Jake had come to help, the car crashed, the window broke, a piece of glass had sliced into Jake's neck. It was a good thing that her dad and Elaine had been too distracted about Eddie to think closely about all the gaps in the story. And after all, Alan *did* have a concussion, Jake's neck *was* badly gashed, and his car *was* in a ditch. It all must have happened somehow.

The shadow of the old willow fell slantwise across Mercy's gravestone. The BROWN was hidden. Only MERCY in bold black letters, was clear.

Haley, kneeling at the grave, thought about Mercy. And about fear.

Had fear been enough to turn Patience into what she was? She'd been so afraid that she wouldn't speak the word *dead* or set foot on a grave. That she'd killed the people closest to her so that her own life could go on.

Was fear all anyone needed? Was that what Patience had meant when she'd told Haley that her own horrible kind of half-life was within Haley's grasp? *You want what I wanted. I know it. For life to go on. Forever.*

No, Haley thought. She didn't want that. Not that. There were worse things than facing the fact that all life had to come to an end. Like living for years and years, alone, with nothing but your hunger for company. Like living forever only because you were scared to death of dying.

Haley stood, backed up a few paces, and slipped her hand into her pocket to find her camera. One last picture. She held the camera out, tilting it to find the best angle.

On the camera's screen, a tiny figure of Mercy looked up at her, still in the long, old-fashioned gray dress with the silver locket around her throat. She smiled and put her arm around the shoulders of a fair-haired little boy. Haley stared at the screen for a moment, wondering if Aunt Nell would make an appearance. But she didn't.

Haley pressed the shutter. Brother and sister, frozen, looked at her for a moment, and then vanished. Now the camera's viewscreen showed nothing but the empty grave.

"Good-bye," Haley whispered.

A car horn blared, making Haley jump. A familiar blue car pulled up at the gate of the cemetery and an arm waved out the window. Mel got out, and then someone climbed out of the driver's side. Alan.

Alan, who had a broken wrist and a concussion and who said he couldn't remember a thing—not seeing Haley on the street, not offering her a ride, not falling down the stairs.

Mel waved again, and Alan walked around to her side of the car, leaning against the hood to wait. He tucked one hand into his pocket. The other, with a cast that went from elbow to knuckles, hung by his side.

Haley's camera was still in her hand. She held it up, tilting it just right to catch both Mel and Alan in the lens. Zoom a little, not too much. The two of them were talking but not looking at each other. Still, they were leaning in just a bit. Haley clicked the shutter once as Mel looked up at Alan, again as she looked quickly away.

Mel put both hands to her mouth and shouted.

"Haley, come *on*! Enough pictures! We're gonna be late!"

Haley had thought it would be just her and Mel. Now what was she? A third wheel? *Go on without me*, Haley thought, and almost shouted it. *Go on, I'll just—*

—just do what? Stay here in a graveyard? Without even ghosts for company?

"Alan said he'd drive," Mel explained, unnecessarily, as Haley reached the gate. She was smiling, tucking a strand of hair back underneath her hat, and talking a little too fast. "And we're picking up Elissa, and Matt and Jonah are meeting us at Starbucks. We could see what's playing at the movies, you want to? And how's Eddie? Is he okay?"

Haley rolled her eyes. "You should hear the racket he makes in the morning."

"And Jake?" Mel's face and voice were genuinely concerned, but her gaze, Haley noticed, kept moving over to Alan.

None of the doctors could explain it, but it was true—Jake was growing stronger. His face had some color in it again. His smile looked the way Haley remembered it. He was talking about going back to school.

Haley had been there, in the hospital room, when her dad had told Jake that Aunt Brown had disappeared. That her old farmhouse was standing empty on its hill.

Jake's eyes had gone to Haley. Once. Then he'd looked away.

And to her surprise, Haley had found she didn't mind all that much. It was okay to have something that she didn't share with Jake. Okay to stand on her own with what she remembered, and what she had done.

"He's pissed," she answered Mel. "He's going to have to quit smoking again."

"Let's put your bike in the back," Alan said. He wore a thin scarf in many shades of green wrapped twice around his neck. His smile was friendly, but no more.

"Sure," Haley answered, unlocking her bike from the fence. "But no horror movies."

Friendly was something. She guessed friendly was fine.

"And no chick flicks." Alan came to help her lift the bike into the back of his car. Since he could only use one hand, he wasn't that much help. Haley didn't have the heart to tell him it would have been easier to do it by herself.

"And no shoot-'em-up cop movies," Mel added.

Alan gave the bike one last shove. "Will you tell me someday?" he asked Haley, too low for Mel to hear. "What really happened?"

Haley looked at him sharply. He'd said he didn't remember. She'd thought that meant spooky stories were one thing, and

171

real vampire hunting was another. That he was like Jake—he didn't want to know.

But maybe that wasn't fair. Alan had been there, right beside her, in that house as quiet and empty as a tomb. He'd seen some of what she'd seen. Patience's room. Mercy.

And he'd believed her. When everyone else—even Jake, even Mel—had thought she was crazy, Alan had believed her.

"Someday," she answered him in the same quiet tone.

Alan gave her a sideways glance and a quick smile. Then he slammed the back door of the car shut. "We may be stuck with a Disney movie," he called out to Mel.

Haley looked out across the cemetery for a moment. She'd never really be on her own, she thought, with the knowledge that Mercy had brought her, and the truth of what Mercy's sister had become. There *were* other people who understood. Some of them could become her friends. Some were even family.

"So let's go!" Mel opened the passenger door. "Come on, Alan. This place gives Haley the creeps."

"No, it doesn't." Haley shook her head. "Not really. Not anymore."

AUTHOR'S NOTE

Mercy Brown of Exeter, Rhode Island, died of tuberculosis (called consumption at the time) in 1892, at the age of nineteen. She was the third of her family to die of the disease, and her brother, Edwin, was very ill with it as well.

Mercy's body, awaiting burial, was placed in a crypt near the graves of her mother and her older sister. Two months after her death, under pressure from friends and neighbors, her father gave permission for the bodies of his wife and daughters to be examined. When Mercy's corpse was cut open, liquid blood was found inside her heart. This was enough proof for the people assembled there. Mercy Brown was still alive, somehow feeding on the life of her dying brother.

Mercy's heart was burned and the ashes were given to Edwin as medicine. It didn't work. Tuberculosis killed Edwin five months after his sister's death.

In my novel, I took the liberty of making Edwin younger than Mercy. The actual Edwin was six years older than his sister. The real Mercy also had four sisters; I changed the number to two and gave them the names Grace and Patience. (And I made the Chestnut Hill Cemetery somewhat larger and more elaborate than it actually is, so that Haley would have a crypt or two to hide behind as Patience hunts her down.)

Other than these changes, Haley's history project tells a true story of a family tragedy and of a desperate attempt on the part of Mercy's family and friends to understand and control a disease that doctors at the time had very little ability to cure. Tuberculosis was both terrifying and baffling. Its victims suffered slow, gruesome deaths and had little hope of survival. The sickness could infect one family while leaving neighbors untouched. As Mercy's story shows, people looked anywhere—even beyond the grave—for an explanation of where the disease came from and for a way to fight it.

If you're interested in more details about the New England vampire tradition, Michael E. Bell's excellent book, *Food for the Dead: On the Trail of New England's Vampires,* is a fascinating read, and Christopher Rondina's *Vampires of New England* is spine-tingling entertainment.

ABOUT THE AUTHOR

S arah L. Thomson has published more than twenty-five books for young readers. A versatile writer, she has created fiction and nonfiction, poetry and prose, fantasy and realism, for age levels from kindergarten through high school. Her books include an adventure about two friends who rescue a dragon's egg, a picture-book biography of Abraham Lincoln, and a young readers' version of the best-selling title, *Three Cups of Tea*, along with poetry for picture-book readers and nonfiction I-Can-Read titles about tigers, whales, sharks, gorillas, and snakes.

Photo by Mark Mattos

The *Washington Post* said that the plot of Sarah's book, *The Manny*, is "worthy of Jane Austen," and *Booklist* called her

Arthurian novel, *The Dragon's Son*, "a spellbinding tale of love, intrigue, and betrayal." Her biography of Abraham Lincoln, *What Lincoln Said*, was reviewed in *People* magazine, and her fantasy novel, *Dragon's Egg*, was the winner of the 2007 Maine Lupine Award.

A former children's book editor for HarperCollins and Simon & Schuster, Thomson now lives in Portland, Maine, with her young daughter and two cats, who help with her writing by lying on the piece of paper she needs most.

Learn more about Sarah's work at *www.sarahlthomson.com*.